Of Jewish Race

A boy on the run in Nazi-occupied Italy

by Renzo Modiano

Translated by
Mirna Cicioni and Susan Walker

Vagabond Voices
Glasgow

Vagabond Voices Publishing Ltd.,
Glasgow,
Scotland.

ISBN 978-1-908251-13-8

Printed and bound in Poland

Cover design by Mark Mechan

Typeset by Park Productions

The publisher acknowledges subsidy towards
this publication from Creative Scotland

For further information on Vagabond Voices, see the website,
www.vagabondvoices.co.uk

In memory of all the children torn from their homes in Rome on the 16th of October 1943

FOREWORD

Some people might be puzzled by the title of this story: "Another book on the Holocaust? So many have already been published. And does it add anything to Primo Levi's writings, to the diaries of the Warsaw Ghetto, or to *The Diary of Anne Frank?*" Undoubtedly, many books have been written about the Holocaust and it is clearly difficult to add anything new to testimonies that everyone is (or ought to be) familiar with.

And yet we keep on writing about that tragedy and will continue to do so. Our astonishment at the horrors carried out by civilised inhabitants of our continent in the so-called "century of progress" has not yet abated, nor will it. If it is true that our curiosity about an event – whether good or evil – is in proportion to its uniqueness and extent, we would need to write at least six million stories in order to pass on to future generations the memory of each life cut short. Each of those lives should be entitled to the dignity of its own story.

Those who survived must narrate and bear witness for the others, for those who were robbed of a voice. Only the author of this book can tell the brief story of Rachel, the blond-haired girl who sat next to him in a primary school "for Jews" in Rome, and who at daybreak would be put on a cattle truck bound for

Auschwitz. Memory is a plant that needs to be nourished, or else it shrivels and dies.

But writing about the persecution suffered by Jews in Italy does not mean having to talk only about atrocities and gas chambers. There were other experiences, which could be described as more "normal", such as the ones in this book: expulsions from state schools, rejection by former school friends, daily humiliations whether small or large. Then came the stress of being on the run and always having to be on the lookout. But then there was also friendship, the discovery of the simplicity of rugged rural life and the generosity of people who, without any personal gain, helped Jews to hide and survive, often running terrible risks for themselves and their families. Italy had many more people like Perlasca1. than one would imagine.

This is a sort of diary written with hindsight, in the simple and spontaneous voice of a seven-year-old boy, whose eyes were naive but perceptive (people mature early in such circumstances). This is the story of how I and the rest of my family experienced and lived through the storm that descended on the Jews of Rome.

One little boy's adventures and thoughts may contribute to the memory of those dark times, a tiny fragment of history which can be added to many others.

1. Giorgio Perlasca (1910-1992), masquerading as a Spanish consular official, managed to smuggle thousands of Hungarian Jews out of Hungary into neutral Spain between 1943 and 1945.

I would like to acknowledge the silent unselfish people who at great risk, possibly of their lives, allowed my family to survive. They never asked for anything, they haven't claimed recognition or rewards; they appeared at the worst time in my life, picked me up and rescued me and, once their mission was accomplished, retreated into the background. My gratitude is a given, but I would like these exceptional people to read their names in the pages of this book.

Renzo Modiano

Of Jewish Race

"Everything a man's blood absorbed from the air around him in childhood remains within him."
                    Stefan Zweig, *The World of Yesterday*

CHAPTER 1

Rome, the 8th of September 1943. I was playing hop-scotch in the street with some other children, when I saw my mother coming. She had a strange expression on her face, which was lit up by a glow of serenity that I had never seen before. Her shortsighted eyes, usually soft and languid, were filled with emotion.

Mamma always walked fast, so it wasn't the speed at which she was coming towards me that made me stop – it was that particular expression on her face. She grabbed my hand and dragged me away, without a thought for my stunned playmates. Whilst I struggled along behind her through the oppressive late-afternoon heat, she said, "Hurry up! We're going home. The war is over!"

I was speechless. That news was much more than a mere surprise. Running along by her side I repeated over and over, "The war's over. The war's over…" I was not quite seven years old and could not understand anything that went beyond my own here and now. I had an inkling that a lot of things around me were about to change, but I could only think about what the changes would mean for me. What was I going to do tomorrow? The end of the war was supposed to be a good thing, but how did a war finish that had started before I could remember?

I hadn't been separated from my father, because being a Jew, he had been deemed unworthy of wearing a soldier's uniform. So what could the end of the war mean? Not my father coming home, as was going to be the case for many of my friends. I suddenly had a thought: they would give us our wireless back. Two plain-clothes policemen had taken it away because we Jews weren't allowed to have one. The end of the war would at least mean that. I lingered over the pleasant prospect, because I had really missed that magical box, which had given me so much to dream about in the short time we'd owned it.

Thoughts come and go quickly, and the way home was long enough for new ones to pop up. War had forever been hanging over our lives. Everyone felt its effects, and the grown-ups talked of nothing else. It permeated everyone's existence: that was why I couldn't grasp the full meaning of its end. I tried to think of other things, but it kept flooding back into my mind, whilst I barely managed to keep up with my mother, who was in more of a hurry than usual that evening.

I'm sure that she would have spoken to me on the walk home, but I can't remember what she said. I kept wondering what peace was like, but I didn't know what it was and had trouble imagining it.

"They won't bomb us anymore," I remember suddenly thinking. I liked the idea, but my pleasure was rather superficial, because I had never really grieved for the victims. The notion I had of them was blurred and only a little more real than my idea of those soldiers who had been killed on the frontline.

Rome had been the target of two heavy air raids, but the bombs hadn't fallen very close to my building. The warning sirens had sounded frequently and we'd often had to run to our air-raid shelter. Going down into that damp cellar had been a diversion and hadn't frightened me. After all, I didn't go on my own, and for a child it's difficult to envisage his home collapsing on top of him whilst he's in his parents' arms. I did hate night-time alarms, though, because they broke my night's sleep. Those raids made me detest the British, because I'd learned that it was their planes that flew at night. The Americans were braver and made their raids in broad daylight. A few times, from the balcony of our flat, I had watched the planes surrounded by puffs of white cloud from the anti-aircraft guns. But the show was usually short-lived, because every single time, my mother would drag me away from my lookout, turning a deaf ear to my protests.

After the two major bombing raids and other less damaging ones along the railway line near our neighbourhood, a curious trade sprang up amongst us children: we found and exchanged bomb shards. They were nearly all so small that the whole lot of them could be held in the palm of your hand. But despite their size, they stayed warm for a long time and were still hot when we picked them up. Those fragments were evidence that the bombs had fallen close to our homes, that is to say, not too far from us, and that filled us with pride. The first time, we had come across them by chance, and were surprised at our find. From then on, as soon as we heard the mournful sound of the "all clear", we rushed out to look for those hot, jagged pieces of metal. Handling them made us feel brave, because it meant that we'd been close to where the bombs had fallen. According to our own peculiar ranking, the child who found the biggest fragment was the bravest, as if he had run the biggest risk in picking it up.

As I tried to imagine the end of the war, I also realised just how much it had been a mystery to me – something I'd given up trying to understand a long time ago and that I'd relegated to a corner of my mind.

One day my parents took me along to have lunch with some friends. "We're celebrating a victory," they said. But during the meal I gleaned from their conversation that in Africa that day it had been the British, not the Italians, who had won. At the time I was surprised, but didn't ask anyone for an explanation, not even my brother and sister, who were both a few years older than me. I didn't doubt my parents' reasons, even though they'd just turned their backs on everything that I'd sincerely believed in up to that moment.

I immediately decided that I would have to solve that mystery on my own, however big it might be. The method I used might not have been very scientific but it gave me more peace of mind. It was based on the certainty that Papà and Mamma were not traitors and therefore must have had very good grounds for thinking as they did. If the whole thing wasn't clear to me, this meant that it was too complicated for me to understand. In any case, I had absolute faith in their loyalty to the Fatherland (that was the word we used and believed in at the time). I had always heard them call Italy "our Fatherland" and say that everyone should love it. There was my mother's brother, Uncle Alberto, who had won a silver medal "in the other war" (I had been so envious of the scar on his chest and had often gone to sleep dreaming that I too, one day, would be wounded and, just like him, be presented with a silver medal by the King himself).

No one in such a family would betray the Fatherland! So it all meant that being loyal was a complicated matter. There had to be some truth, too, in the words I had so often heard: "Children can't understand everything that goes on around them!" There was another thing. Even though my parents had carefully avoided discussing politics while I was around, they hadn't been able to avoid letting something slip every once in a while – the odd joke, for instance – that showed that in their minds there was a difference between the Fatherland and Fascism. It was inevitable that this would happen, since both of them had been members of the Socialist Party for years and at home it was natural for everyone to say what they thought. So, from their occasional unguarded comments I had understood that Italy was one thing and Fascism, that governed it, was another. Even though I didn't know what "govern" meant. After that lunch, I got used to living with this strange contradiction, which was far from simple. I gave myself two rules: to listen to as much as I could and not to ask questions. I'd realized that there were some things one mustn't talk about.

All of us were very tense, as they were in every Italian home that evening. During dinner, I tried hard to understand what was being said by Papà, Mamma and Aunt Amelia, my father's sister, who lived with us. I didn't really follow what they were talking about, but they weren't as happy as I expected them to be. What was wrong? After all they had said against the war, why wasn't peace cheering them up? A new mystery to add to the others.

Papà made one phone call after another, using a language that was incomprehensible to me and every time he hung up, he was more agitated than before. Every time he mentioned the Germans, the two furrows between his eyebrows got deeper – a sign of profound worry and apprehension. Eventually, my mother sent me off to bed, later than normal because she had forgotten my bedtime and I had been careful not to do anything to remind her of it.

Next day things were still in turmoil at home, and Mamma and Aunt Amelia were agitated, to say the least – a good reason to keep out of their way and enjoy the unexpected freedom they were allowing me. Just before lunchtime there was a ring at the doorbell. It was Signor Pirani, who lived two floors below us. Pirani was a Fascist Party official, but his friendly manner towards us had not changed after the race laws came into force. Papà spent a few minutes with him in the study, whilst all of us, even my mother, cast anxious glances towards the closed door. Pirani wasn't in the habit of dropping in, which meant that this wasn't just a neighbourly visit. At last, Papà and Pirani came out of the study. As he saw him out, my father with both hands warmly took the right hand of the other man, who had often made me feel uneasy and frightened when he was decked out in one of the Fascist regime's extravagant uniforms.

Once the visitor was gone, we crowded round my father to ask him the reason for the unexpected visit. Pirani had come to warn us: the Germans were about to enter Rome. "Unfortunately, they really mean it about the Jews," Pirani had said. Papà now repeated it word for word, without worrying about the effect it might have on us, not even on me. I didn't really understand what it all meant, but it shook me. What did *we* have to do with the Germans? And yet…the look that passed between my parents, and which I still remember, was a further warning of what lay ahead of us.

When I woke up the next morning on the 10th of September, Papà had gone out and Mamma was clearly worried about him. Why is she fretting like this, I wondered, he goes out every day. Whatever could happen to him? Especially now we're at peace and nobody is going to bomb us! I'd forgotten all about Pirani. Apparently, peace didn't bring quiet. Every now and again I stopped playing in order to take a peep at what my mother was doing. She was still agitated and inevitably she took out some of her tension on me. From late morning on, we began to hear the strange noise of thunder in the distance. But it wasn't thunder, I guessed, even though the sky was overcast and it looked like rain. My mother's replies to my questions were unusually evasive. But there was something else: her words hinted bitterly at a threat that was vague and therefore all the more insidious and unsettling. I no longer remember them exactly, but I remember that they made me very afraid.

Around half past one, my father came home and I heard him say that some people were fighting against the Germans to defend Rome. That day our lunch was very gloomy. At the crowded table, Mamma didn't dish out portions as was her habit, and there was none of the usual mealtime chatter. Only Papà spoke and he did so in an unusually forceful and tense way. Mamma didn't interrupt him and just listened, uncharacteristically submissive. We were affected by an ominous silence. We ate without a fuss and that alone showed just how unnatural and sinister that silence was.

The three of us children – Guido, Elena and I – kept quiet as did our cousin Yvonne, Aunt Amelia's daughter, who was older than us. We exchanged nervous, puzzled looks. No great insight was required to tell that it was no time for joking, even though we didn't have the slightest idea what was going on around us. Suddenly, as if he'd only just remembered us, Papà said, "Children, we have to leave the flat now. We won't be able to stay together. We must leave immediately because the Germans are entering Rome and they're taking the Jews."

"They're taking the Jews." This expression – vague, understated and incomplete, was even less comprehensible than anything I had heard up to that moment, but its effect on me was tangible and more cutting than the lash of a whip. "We will have to split up and live in different places," Papà was saying. Everything that I was used to was going to disappear, as if by magic: people, home, things, all my world. I was stunned and couldn't take in the meaning of his words. How could I have done?

The race laws had taught me that I was different from other people. I'd suffered occasional hurt and humiliation from the kids I played with in the street, but how could we live anywhere else but home? Most importantly, what did "the Germans are taking the Jews" mean? The full scope of that understatement would continue to amaze me after the war ended, when everything was revealed and when – at great human cost – the horror was over. In what better way could the impending tragedy have been communicated? Without being explicit, those words hinted at a fatal threat. "They're taking the Jews" conveyed only the first step, but allowed a glimpse of the journey that would follow – right to the end.

At that time, anyone who wanted to "know" knew. Only the most atrocious details of the extermination might have remained unknown. My father was one of those people who could not turn a blind eye to what was going on. That's why, during the months that followed, when we wanted to exorcise the unbearable meaning of the threat, we never used words that were more explicit than "They're taking the Jews." Those words did not rule out the possibility of a return.

So we had to get away and go separately – five of us and Aunt Amelia with Yvonne. Less than two hours later, while the guns at Porta San Paolo still roared, we left our home, under a leaden and menacing sky. The dining table was still partly covered with dishes and the flat was a long way from being as tidy as my mother liked to see it. In my whole life, even in films, I have never seen an escape scene more telling than those dishes left on the tablecloth still covered in crumbs from the last piece of bread.

CHAPTER 2

The previous year I had started going to school, moving straight into second grade. I accessed the education system of the Kingdom of Italy by the back door, attending the inconvenient afternoon sessions reserved for Jews. This was a Fascist ruling that was more painful for our parents than for us, because Saturday afternoons were decreed to be holidays, in addition to us having Sundays off.

Evil deeds sometimes work against those who conceive them. The Fascist desire to isolate and stifle the Jewish community produced an extraordinary situation where Jewish culture became stronger. In normal times, State education would never have extended its curriculum, as had been done by the Fascist regime, to teach the ancestral language and religion of barely one in a thousand Italians. But what matters is *how* things are obtained, more than what those things actually are: under the circumstances, the fact that we were studying Hebrew did not please our parents in the least.

At first, I thought the Hebrew language was fun: it seemed to be the opposite of my own and while I shakily copied out its characters I felt as if I were playing a sort of "mirror game". I liked Hebrew despite the fact that our teacher, a refugee from who knows where, did nothing to lighten up the lessons as they got gradually more challenging. I wasn't all that willing to make any allowances for his gloominess either (he never smiled), although there must have been a reason for it. Back then I couldn't have understood what that was, but now when I think about his eyes, I recognise the devastation of someone who has already seen too much too early. Besides, sadness didn't only hover around him. It had taken root between those walls and wrapped itself around us, too.

In all the school years that came after the war, I can remember being scared of being picked on by the teacher to answer questions, but I also remember great bursts of laughter and outbreaks of infectious giggling, nearly always for no good reason at all, and always liberating. I can't remember one single such moment of collective joy in the year 1942-43. We were estranged from the world around us and relying on the support of parents who were insecure and humiliated.

I was in a mixed grade and our class teacher kept the boys and girls separate. Since there was an odd number of each, she had to establish a desk on the border, for one boy and one girl. I was selected for that desk. I had to sit next to a girl and I wasn't happy about it at all. Like all boys of that age I was a hardhearted misogynist. "I don't play with dolls," I thought. For a while, whenever I wasn't looking at the teacher, I kept my head turned towards my own kind.

The girl I had to sit next to was called Rachel. She was slim, blonde and blue-eyed, but at the beginning of the year I didn't care what she looked like. Her background wasn't Italian – her grandparents had come from a central European country, whose name I forget. She often said things in that language, which made me cross because I didn't understand, but she thought it was funny. It was her weapon and she used it against me when she thought I'd done something wrong.

At first we all but ignored each other. Then slowly we were forced to talk, sharing as we did one of the hard wooden black and grey cages that were our school desks in those days. "Do you want a pen nib?" "Can you give me some ink?" "May I borrow your rubber?" "Watch out, you've got all dirty!" which she often said to me. Simple exchanges; but then as time went on, the daily difficulties of school work meant that we started to help each other, even whispering the right answers. Our first meeting ground was the correct spelling of the occasional word, but it was over the times tables, which we took turns testing each other on, that the ice started to thaw. Little by little I began to appreciate her being different, without being able to define in what way. I didn't wonder why her difference intrigued me. I liked it and that was enough for me. As the school year progressed, when I didn't have to look at the teacher, I found I was turning less and less to the boys' side of the room.

One day Rachel asked me to a birthday party in her home. I was flattered to be the only classmate invited, apart from another boy who lived next door to her. It didn't occur to me that it was only because I was the boy sitting beside her. I preferred to think that she had chosen me after a careful selection process. I already knew Rachel's mother because she used to come and collect her after school, but I'd never seen her father before and I only caught a glimpse of him that day. We had fun at her party. I can't remember what we played, since there were no toys at her place. This was usual in those days, unless the family was very, very wealthy. On my way home, still happy and excited, I made my mother promise that we would invite Rachel to my birthday party. I would have to wait a long time, because my birthday had just passed.

"I'll invite her next year," I said to myself, thinking about the next school year, rather than calendar year.

It might seem strange these days, but I wouldn't have had other chances to see Rachel outside school. Those were definitely not times when people gave parties, unless on special occasions, at least birthdays. After school, she went home in one direction and I in the other.

I walked home with a friend from a wealthier family. They had a German nanny, Jewish of course, because we weren't allowed to have Aryan help. I can't remember her name; I recall that she was very slight, with a waif-like figure, closer to our childish bodies than to an adult's one. We ignored her as we walked and she did no more than keep an eye on us at a distance. If we stopped to look at something, or lingered too long, she'd call out, "Schnell, schnell, *Faccetta!*" (*Faccetta* was the nickname my friend's family had given him).[2] That pet name together with the stern German word made me laugh. At school I had fun saying it too, "Schnell, schnell, *Faccetta.*" Then we would both giggle behind our hands.

---

2. *Faccetta* – The nickname (literally: "little face") refers to the popular song *Faccetta nera*, written at the time of the Fascist colonial war in Ethiopia (1935-36), where an Italian soldier patronisingly calls an Abyssinian girl "little black face" and tells her that she will become Italian under Mussolini.

Our way home was along Via Nomentana, which in those days was splendid. Two pedestrian paths, covered in gravel, with carefully tended flower beds, ran along either side of the main avenue, where the traffic was sparse. Leafy tree branches hung over them and hid the sky from the cars too. In autumn the ground where people walked was covered in leaves that *Faccetta* and I enjoyed kicking. Messing up the natural pattern of the yellow and brown carpet that spread under our feet gave us an intoxicating sense of power and had a liberating effect after the stress of long hours of captivity at our school desks.

Plain-clothes police officers were stationed in front of Villa Torlonia, where the *Duce* lived. They walked up and down beside the wall that surrounded the villa. They were there night and day, ready to question any adult who stopped anywhere near that wall. They were dressed in black and wore hats.

Once a week, as we walked home we would come across soldiers returning from the changing of the guard at the Quirinale.3. Heading for their barracks, which were beyond our homes, they marched to the rhythm of a band and its drums. *Faccetta* and I were entranced by the drum major, who waved a huge, shining baton with a virtuoso skill we found miraculous, and we had fun trying to imitate them. The maestro twirled his baton and threw it into the air whilst marching, every catch winning our gasps and boundless admiration.

---

3. *Quirinale* – One of the Seven Hills of Rome, where the residence of the Italian Head of State is located. The King of Italy, Victor Emmanuel III, lived there until the 9th of September 1943, when he fled Rome before the Germans entered the city.

On those afternoons, the nanny didn't need to shout her "schnell" to push *Faccetta* and me along. She was the one who struggled to keep up with us, as we followed the marching soldiers, envious of them, as were all little boys in those years full of war rhetoric.

CHAPTER 3

My father had to hide six people on the day we left home. He immediately took care to spread us out, not letting any of us know the whereabouts of the others. He was the only one who knew everyone's hiding place. I didn't stay long in my first hideout – barely a week. General Sascaro, who was sheltering me and my sister, worked at Army Headquarters, and he too had to hide from the Germans. At the end of a week my mother came to take me away.

It was afternoon when she turned up to collect me. She had brought me a travelling bag that seemed big to me at the time. It was leather, like a doctor's bag, with a sliding lock on top of the metal band that ran the length of the bag. It had a rigid, semi-circular handle. I guessed that I was about to go on a journey, and my whole body was electrified with excitement. A journey, no matter how short, was an event in those days. I said a hasty goodbye to my hosts, who were understandably busy dealing with the problem of their own flight.

Once outside, Mamma said, "Tonight you're going away with Guido. You're going to Abruzzo where you'll stay until Papà and I come and get you."

"When are you going to come?"

"Soon I hope…In any case, we'll come and see you."

"But who am I going to stay with in Abruzzo... Where *is* Abruzzo?"

"With a friend, Signor Lanzi. You're going to like it in the country and you'll have a good time. Lanzi has a boy of your age."

"But who is Lanzi and how are Guido and I going to get there? Are you taking us?"

"Lanzi is a caretaker that Papà knows. And d'you know, he's also a watchmaker. One of his relatives will take you there."

She hesitated for a moment before adding, "They're expecting you." The hesitation was because my mother didn't know how to lie.

As I listened to her I felt two conflicting emotions: leaving her frightened me – the reasons for the journey were serious and we weren't just going on a holiday. But I was also drawn by the suggestion of adventure. I was going to live in the country, where I'd never been. I was going with Guido, who was nearly six years older than me, and who could be an acceptable stand-in for my parents, or my father at least. In addition, my mother had made no mention of school and something told me that I wouldn't have to go to one in the place we were headed for. That was not to be underrated. If it hadn't been for that palpable sense of danger and the hint of tears in my mother's eyes, I would have been happy.

We went to get Guido. Mother turned to him immediately and gave him a quick lesson on how to behave as a guest in the home of others: "Try not to impose, don't ask for anything that you're not offered... Always say thank you." I too was given a condensed lesson in manners – all in the space of a few minutes, as we made our way to meet the person who was going to take us there.

She let loose a veritable torrent of motherly advice on Guido and me. It rained down on us briefly and heavily, like the summer storm that was threatening to soak Rome that evening. Her advice came thick and fast because she wasn't prepared for what was happening: nobody in our family had anticipated splitting up and my mother had never expected to have to entrust her children to strangers.

Suddenly Mamma took a letter out of her handbag and gave it to Guido, telling him that it was for Signor Lanzi: "Make sure you give it to him as soon as you get there." My brother slipped it into the inside pocket of his jacket. I knew it was from my father as I recognised his handwriting on the envelope. Then she started again with her dos and don'ts, which were beginning to bore me because I thought I'd learned everything about living in other people's houses: "Be good. Do as you're told. Remember that you are guests." And finally, to Guido, "Make sure you take good care of Renzo."

Just as it was getting dark and after climbing on and off several trams, we arrived at the meeting place. My mother didn't know who was supposed to take us, and it turned out to be a teenage girl, barely older than Guido. Until the girl stood in front of us, my mother had no idea, but they must have used a signal to recognise each other. The girl looked frightened and confused among the crowd that filled the square. On seeing her, Mamma couldn't hide her dismay. I could read it in her eyes and feel it through her hand gripping mine as if to hold me back, as if she were refusing to deliver me into the care of such a fragile and inexperienced guardian.

Our guide looked as if she needed protection herself – more than she would have been able to give Guido and me. And any journey in those days was risky, as our short journey to Abruzzo proved to be for us.

Having to leave my mother behind made me sad, but I couldn't help feeling a little thrill. "Anyway, she'll soon come to see me," I kept reassuring myself. We had to take a tram to get to the station we were leaving from. Naturally I gave my mother a hug before getting on, but once I'd climbed aboard I felt the need to see her one more time. I leaned out from the top of the steps (it was a tram with no doors) to see her once more and blow her another kiss.

A moment later, I'd forgotten that last goodbye. My mother, on the other hand, was really affected by it. She recalled it later, every time (and there were many) she told the story of the day we left. She always said that it "broke her heart" when she saw me reappear on the tram steps; she feared that the image of me travelling off and blowing her "that extra kiss" would be the last she ever saw of her youngest child. She worried that a premonition I would never see her again had prompted me to add one further farewell. The truth was that I'd only wanted to say goodbye again before setting off on our adventure.

Three hours later we were still unhappily stranded among the rubble of Tiburtina Station, squashed into an overcrowded carriage on a stationary train. Any mention of timetables in those days would have been absurd and no one had any idea when the train would leave. Every now and then somebody, who had heard it from someone equally misinformed, said that the train was about to move off – but it never did. I began to doubt that it ever would and felt scared that we would be made to get off and return to where we had come from. Where would I go back to? Neither Guido nor I knew the whereabouts of our parents or other family members, or anyone else we could go and stay with. I looked at the girl and wondered if she would take us home with her. She did have a home and wasn't on the run like us. But then, how would we find Mamma and Papà again? I started to feel uneasy and my only comfort was the hope that the train would eventually get going. The uneasiness gradually turned into fear. I managed to keep it to myself though. I wasn't going to be the first to give in.

Luckily, the situation I found myself in absorbed a lot of my attention. I was wedged together with lots of strangers, packed like sardines, on a muggy summer evening. My pride and good manners prevented me from complaining; the three of us were probably the only people who didn't. I kept quiet, immersed in the amazing experience. I felt like a piece that didn't fit in, among a crowd of so many human beings who were different from me; so many more than I had ever seen in such a small space. People who were powerless and bad-tempered, waiting for a normal event like the departure of a train, which looked like it might not happen at all. They were all talking in a language that was hard to understand4. and quite different from mine. I could barely grasp the meaning of what they were saying or make out a whole sentence. I was surprised at discovering this other language in my own city. All I understood

---

4. Until the 1950s the main language spoken by the majority of the Italian population was the local dialect. Some dialects are very different from the standard language.

was that they were talking about food, their fear, the war that was over and yet didn't seem to be over …and about the train that just wouldn't get going.

It took an air-raid siren to finally get us out of the station. The train moved slowly as if it really didn't mean to, travelling half-heartedly like that for more than an hour before reaching a station. We arrived at Orte. Here it looked as if the sluggish train was going to make another long stop. For several minutes we couldn't hear any of the usual noises a train makes before it leaves, like the engine puffing harder or the doors of the carriages being slammed shut.

Once again it was planes that forced us to move.

We heard them overhead, just preceded by the wail of an air-raid siren. Immediately afterwards we heard blasts as bombs fell on the station around us. Then the train did set off at full steam, through the flashes and clouds of smoke. For a while we were able to look back and see the darkness lit by explosions and fire bombs. When the train rounded a bend and it all disappeared from view, the dull echo of the blasts continued for a long time.

It was the middle of the night when my tiredness finally overcame the excitement and emotion of that day, and I fell asleep, sitting on the floor. The turmoil of a crowd exasperated and terrified by the bomb raids was very different from staying up late for a family event at home. My sleep was destined to be brief, however. A couple of gunshots were heard just before the train jolted to a stop. People cried out, frightened by the sudden, sharp braking. When the train stopped and nothing happened, nobody felt reassured. An unnatural calm settled over everyone: the silence that ran through the train felt ominous and full of tension. Then, slowly, whispering started to fill the uncomfortable shared space of our third-class carriage, which was open and not divided into compartments. Very soon the whispering rose to a din. Nobody could figure out who had fired the shots or why.

Finally, a couple of brave souls stuck their heads out of the carriage window, which was close to the engine. They were able to see that the drivers were conferring with three shadowy figures standing beside the tracks. But the content of the conversation was still a mystery, because the men on the ground were Germans. Everyone created their own version of what was being said and explained what they had worked out. Words passed along the carriage like a silly parlour game of Chinese whispers played by exhausted, confused people. It was obvious that this was the way they were venting their frustration at being stationary yet again, in the middle of the night in the open countryside, without knowing why, or for how long they would be stuck in that infuriating situation.

In the end, one way or another, the correct version of events filtered through: the German patrol had fired off warning shots because the station at Terni, which we were about to pull into, was being bombed. Yet another wait, and another burst of comments. Many people thanked the heavens for our third lucky escape. Only after everyone resigned themselves to the wait and stopped chattering, could we hear the echoes of the explosions, coming from ahead this time instead of behind.

We were stationary for some time and in the end even the adults gave in to their tiredness and slept.

By then, they had given up any hope of spending the remainder of the night in the place they had planned to arrive.

Without my realising it, in the first light of dawn the train moved off again and cautiously pulled into the town of Terni. I awoke when it stopped. The station was enveloped in smoke and some fires were still burning. An engine had been split in half and the two pieces, pointing to the sky, were vomiting the last of the steam left in the shattered boiler. Now and again, someone appeared and then disappeared in the smoke and uncertain light of day. A handful of shadows drifted about for no apparent reason. If I had already been familiar with Dante's *Inferno*, I would certainly have been reminded of the lost souls in one of the circles of Hell.

In Orte a few hours earlier, the bombs had fallen not far from us, but here the impact of war was greater. Its effects were in front of my eyes, and the scene was much more eloquent than any of the many words I had heard spoken. Just by reaching out I could have touched some of the red-hot debris left by the bomb. I was breathing in smoke from the burning fires and at any moment I might have seen the body of someone who had been killed.

The idea of looking for bomb fragments did not enter my head. I was dazed, aware that I would never forget what I was seeing at that moment – all the details being taken in by the sharp and rapid gaze of my eyes freed from sleep as if by magic. Perhaps there were casualties that night, but luckily I was spared the sight of them.

My brother and the girl were dazed and bewildered, too. None of us found the words to comment on what we were seeing. We silently pointed out to one another the things that most shocked us. In the light of day, the station began to wake up. We could see that the main building was still standing, although damaged and still smouldering here and there. To our amazement we noticed that life was resuming inside. At that point, our guide left to go and find something warm to drink (we had a few sandwiches with us) and to ask what train we would have to take to our destination.

Predictably, the refreshment stand wasn't open, but more importantly, she found out that later on a train would be leaving for where we were headed. We had our doubts, because in the scene of devastation we couldn't see any engines in working condition, and it seemed unlikely that anything could set off from the ruined station. But we hadn't taken into account *our* engine, which pulled our train out of there a few hours later. At about two in the afternoon, after a last, slow stretch without incident, the three of us got off at a tiny station two or three kilometres from Civitatomassa, the village where we were going.

Tired, sleepy and weighed down by our luggage, we had to walk all the way to the village, because no one had come to meet us.

CHAPTER 4

No one was waiting for us for the simple reason that no one had been told we were coming. Lanzi, the caretaker in one of the apartment blocks my father managed, had gone home in August to tend the little piece of land he owned. My father, who had never been a pushy man, had decided that Lanzi would be the one to look after Guido and me. This presumptuousness was justified by the desperate situation and the fact that my father knew Lanzi well and had experienced his great generosity.

As it was, my father sent us there without any prior warning, but how could he have done otherwise? In 1943, contacting Civitatomassa by phone was out of the question. So in order to ask Lanzi to look after us boys, for as long as was necessary, there was no other way but to send a letter after the fact – the one our mother had given Guido the evening before. The Lanzis welcomed us as if we were two grandchildren visiting their country villa. But the house was no villa, having only two rooms. If our father had known, he might not have been so bold as to impose our presence on them; even less so if he had foreseen that our hosts would give Guido and me their own room and even their bed, making do with mattresses rolled out on the kitchen floor, where their son Gabriele also slept. There was no way of refusing their overwhelming hospitality.

The village of Civitatomassa was a cluster of houses where little more than two hundred souls lived. Illiteracy was the norm, and you could have counted those who could read on the fingers of two hands. The Lanzis' house, like all the others, was without electric light, running water or a toilet. For our bodily needs, there was a pigsty across an open courtyard. There was no paper of any description and so leaves took its place for hygienic purposes. I thanked my lucky stars that our stay coincided with autumn, a season in which the primary material was abundant.

The village had two fountains where water was pumped into large copper pitchers. It was the women's job to fetch it for the house on their heads, a full jug at a time that sat on a ring of twisted cloth. It was a wonderful sight to see them pass, straight-backed and confident as queens, wearing shoes that were falling apart on cobbled paths often slippery with rain. I never saw a pitcher fall or any water splash over the rim.

Life in that tiny hamlet was the same as it had been in 1843, or in 1743, or even further back in time. The only difference was that from the highest point in the village you could make out a train in the distance. Once a day it crawled uphill and once a day it ran down, hugging the mountain side, appearing and disappearing among the ridges.

The economy of the town was based on every family being self-sufficient: I never saw money in all the time I was there, but watched many an exchange. I also came to know some of the exchange rates established between the goods being traded, which were only foodstuffs. The communal oven was fired two or three times a month to bake bread dough made at home. In addition, the women made large, thin *focacce*, seasoned only with oil and salt. On those days the smell wafted through the village for hours and the kids pawed the ground like colts while waiting for their mothers to come out of the bakery. Nothing could be quite as delicious as that *focaccia* straight out of the oven. Even today, every time I enter a bakery I long to recapture that taste, but am always disappointed.

The women had a thousand jobs to do that did not finish when the sun went down. They worked longer hours than the men, who were responsible for the work on the land. Men's work was heavier but its rhythm was slower and broken by long pauses. Every family had a vegetable garden, hens, a couple of pigs, a small plot sown with wheat and sweet corn, and one or two fruit or olive trees. A few of them, the richest, also had one or two cows. This was the way they had lived and survived for centuries. While I was discovering the rituals, gestures and secrets of that peasant culture, little did I know that I was watching the demise of a way of life that had its origins in the dim and distant past.

September had gone and October was passing in days full of wonder. Country life had not yet exhausted its repertoire of surprises and experiences. There was still much we could be part of, in addition to the grape harvest. In the country there are countless tasks to be carried out in preparation for winter – countless but not endless. We had more and more time to try and fill as the days became shorter and darker. The only toy that I had brought from home was a propeller. It consisted of an iron rod about twenty centimetres long with a thread running up its length, an empty tin cylinder and a small tin propeller. We put the propeller on top of the cylinder then pushed it up as hard as we could. The thread on the rod made the propeller spin and take off. The longer the propeller stayed up the better the player was. It was easy to lose the propeller: a gust of wind could blow it too far or send it who knows where. All too soon, this happened to mine. My only toy was blown away.

I was left with only my imagination for entertainment. The three of us, the boys from Rome, found it difficult to play with the other kids (I say "the three of us" because Gabriele, too, was seen as an outsider by the village kids). In those days there was a vast cultural gap between the ways of a big city and the ways of a tiny village in the country. To begin with, we spoke different languages. Gabriele helped us but sometimes even he found the local dialect difficult to understand. How can you play with someone who doesn't understand you straight away? No one feels like consulting an interpreter in the middle of a game. For a long time language was a barrier between us and the other children, reinforcing the deep-rooted mistrust that country folk felt towards city folk.

"*Temè, Temè!*" a couple of them shouted to me one day. Eventually from their gestures I understood that they were telling me to look at something in the distance. "Look over there, look over there!" They had not, as I immediately suspected, made up the words on the spur of the moment to tease me. Children, more conformist than grown-ups because of their overriding need for the familiar, tend to exclude outsiders, so the three of us often ended up on our own for whole days at a time.

The Lanzis were left out too. I had noticed that no one dropped in and they rarely visited anyone either, even though they were related to several of the village people. Probably the fear that Guido and I might do something to give ourselves away reinforced their natural tendency to keep to themselves. To be honest, other families did not often go out visiting either. Coming from Rome, when I first set eyes on that cluster of houses and smattering of people, my first impression was that they were one big harmonious extended family. To my amazement I soon found out that there was no harmony at all. Quite the opposite, a silent resentment between family groups divided the village. That resentment appeared to be ancient, born who knows when and who knows why. It gave no sign of changing, whether for better or for worse, or of coming to a head. It was constant and could be detected in the stubborn silences in that tiny community, where every day at dawn everyone set out towards their own bit of land to tend to their own affairs.

I was very surprised by those divisions but I never asked Lanzi what had brought them about for fear of prying (I remembered my mother's instructions). My tentative explanation for the absence of people chatting in the deserted streets was that everyone was too busy surviving to have the time or energy to pay social calls. They only ever came together when there was a reason to do so, that is, when they could not avoid it – for the grape harvest, or wine-making, or hunting. The women had a few more opportunities to meet, at the fountains where they drew water and did the washing, or at the communal oven while waiting for the bread to bake.

Children did not visit each other either and I only went inside other people's houses on two or three occasions, so even playing was not simple. This was a significant problem for me, because it is a small step from being bored to being sad. I soon found out that the only way to avoid giving in to gloomy thoughts was to keep busy.

In my daily quest for entertainment I received unexpected help from the rain, which turned the earth into lots of wonderful clay. I spent hours and hours making things out of it. One day I put all my energy into making a ship, a beautiful, big one, with cannons aimed upwards in tiered gun turrets. I was really proud of it and I had to show it to someone beside Guido and Gabriele, who had been stingy with their praise (in my opinion they were jealous).

An elderly lady went by; I knew her, like I knew everyone by then.

"Signora, see what I've made?" (I didn't use the polite Italian form of address, which she wouldn't have understood).[5.]

"Don't know. What is it?" she asked in dialect.

"What d'you mean, what is it? Can't you see?"

The old lady took another look at my skilful creation and after a slight hesitation said in dialect, "A shoe?"

"It's *not* a shoe," I replied, "Can't you see? Tell me what it is!" (Being upset, I had slipped into the most familiar form of address).

Now it was the old lady's turn to be annoyed, "How should I know – a shoe," she pronounced, turning her back on me and going on her way.

---

5. Italian has three forms of address: the polite *Lei*, the old-fashioned polite *voi*, and the very familiar *tu*. Renzo first uses *voi* and then *tu*.

I was furious. How could she ignore the evidence before her eyes? It was only later that the penny dropped: the old lady could never have recognised something she did not know. There is no sea anywhere near Civitatomassa, and she would never have picked up a book or a newspaper. So where could she have ever seen a ship? She was bound to have heard of ships, given that so many immigrants from Abruzzo had travelled the world, but who knows how an elderly woman like her would have imagined one. She wouldn't even have seen that many shoes.

Shoes were a constant worry in those years, a problem that became more and more serious as time went by. There was no material to make clothes either, but the lack of shoes was felt more keenly. Clothes could be turned, cut down to fit younger children or altered in a variety of ways, but shoes could not. When their time came, it was the end – the leather gave out and the soles were little more than stiffened cardboard.

What was the most important selling point for a shoe? – that it had been made before the war. But the shoe salesmen lied, because for a long time all that was left of pre-war shoes was the memory. This gave rise to cork-soled shoes for women and wooden clogs for everyone, especially children. Clogs were to shoes as mules were to horses. They were humble, slow, not much to look at but solid, and they suited the extraordinary stresses to which children subject shoes. Clogs were our means of transport, and shoes our luxury vehicles to be used only on Sundays. Luckily I had my clogs in my suitcase; the shoes I was wearing when I left Rome wouldn't have lasted a week subjected to the dust, mud and stones in the lanes of Civitatomassa. They were the classic clog: a wooden base with a central strip of leather from which three cross-strips branched off to the left and right, like the legs of a spider. A strap with a buckle on it was threaded through two thin leather loops at ankle height and ran round the back of the heel to stop the foot lifting too much.

A classic, as I said, that caused me all the problems typical of the style. When a group of kids was playing, there was always someone who had to pull out, lamed by the breakdown of a clog. They would sit there fixing it while the others played on regardless. The first thing you had to do was find a flat stone suitable for driving in the tacks that kept the straps attached to the wood. Sometimes we had no tacks on us and had to ask a friend for some, to avoid going home with the risk of being kept there. Some of the smarter boys took the precaution of putting a few in their pockets before coming out in preparation for the likely event. The problem was more serious when the leather or the wooden sole had been mended so many times that they gave out and fell apart. When that happened the strap had to be replaced and that was a job for an adult, a mother or a father. You could temporarily ignore a cross-strap coming unstuck, but the increased strain on the other two would cause them to break as well in a very short time. So it was wise to take action immediately and that's what we did.

This "mule" needed constant attention, and the first manual work carried out by kids in those times was work done on clogs. Repairing them was such a test of one's skills that these days it would be called an aptitude test. By today's standards, a fair assessment would have placed me among the less able apprentices. I always ended up losing my temper when I was "lamed", and for this reason I have never had a happy relationship with that means of transport. Perhaps my dislike of sandals stems from these memories. As soon as I was able to choose, I veered without hesitation towards lace-ups.

One morning, while getting dressed, I had a horrible surprise. One of the cross-straps of a clog had disappeared. There were remnants of leather under the tacks, some attached to the central strap, but nothing in between.

I cast a suspicious eye on my brother, who was innocently getting dressed too. Had he played a nasty trick on me? No, that wasn't like him, I thought. Not even if he'd wanted to get back at me for something. But get back at me for what? The night before we hadn't even had a fight. Gabriele? No, even less likely.

"Guido, look at my clog. Whatever can have happened?"

My brother glanced at the clog, "You must have broken it".

"No, I'm telling you, it wasn't broken when I went to bed last night and anyway, how could it break like this?"

That made Guido take a bit more notice, but there was no way we could come up with a plausible explanation. Even Lanzi, who replaced the strap by dipping into his precious little hoard of spare leather, wasn't able to find one. We all thought of rats but they had an alibi: no one in living memory had ever heard of them eating bits of shoes or clogs. Not even in wartime. The "incident" occurred again a few days later involving one of Guido's clogs, which made him much more interested in the problem. The criminal used the same *modus operandi*: the strap had been torn off, all the way to the tacks.

One night I woke up and heard a strange noise. With all the speed I could muster I silently lit the candle on the bedside table. The rabbit that we had got a few days before was happily dining on a clog. We kept him inside only at night to protect him from the cold, so we overlooked him in our search for the culprit. Damaging a clog was a serious crime. It robbed someone of their means of getting around, so the punishment had to be serious. Mamma Lanzi, who had always pictured the rabbit in the pot rather than in the house, requested the death penalty. Lanzi was reluctant, because he had secretly enjoyed the diversion. The three of us defended the rabbit with all our might, saying we would refuse to eat him anyway.

We managed to save him, but it was only a stay of execution. A few nights later (the clogs carefully hidden away), we were woken up by a mysterious noise, like a loud hiss. In a second we were all on our feet with candles in our hands. As we walked we felt something tiny and crunchy under our feet. The rabbit had gnawed through the cloth of a full sack of grain, which had spurted out over the floor like water from a new spring. It took us ages to scoop it all up the next day, and with every minute that passed our hopes of saving the rabbit a second time dwindled. There could be no appeal, even though no one had explicitly passed sentence, and Mamma Lanzi found a way of getting round our repeated refusals to eat our pet. When we came back home late morning, the rabbit had disappeared. That evening, in the pot on the edge of the large fireplace, a large piece of beef was simmering in a rich broth.

An exchange had been made and we knew with whom: one of the peasants had just slaughtered a cow.

CHAPTER 5

While I was worrying about my precious clogs, Lieutenant Colonel Adolf Eichmann was worrying about his career. He wanted to be promoted to Standartenführer, *the next rank in the SS. His friends' careers were progressing faster than his. And yet, his dedication to his work was at least equal to theirs. He was skilled at his job as a "shipping agent" dealing in human flesh (his "pieces" as he called what he was dispatching) and he always carried out his duties with an attention to detail that verged on the obsessive.*

The problem was that his work was lowly and could have been done by a second-rate public servant. It was beset with practical difficulties too: the war effort meant a constant shortage of rolling stock. Added to that, people frequently obstructed him on one pretext or another. Among his opponents, there was still the odd (though rare) person who felt an anachronistic moral hostility towards his mission to clean up Europe. In the Department of Foreign Affairs, for instance, there were people who objected to his shipments of Jewish citizens of neutral countries – as if Jews anywhere were not the Reich's worst enemies. In Denmark, the Resistance had spirited away hundreds of "pieces" right under his nose, ferrying them to Sweden over a couple of nights with any craft they could get their hands on. Even in France, which had a government that collaborated with the Reich, elements within the police force had secretly warned

Jews on the day before a round-up, so that many of the condemned escaped the fate that had been planned for them. To say nothing of Bulgaria, where the King and government had opposed any deportation – and so the Jews remained, unaware of the plan he had laid to take them all away. Because that was his job, his duty to history: to cleanse every corner of Europe of the Jewish cancer.

No, in spite of his commitment, he had to admit that he had not produced the results his superiors expected. He could understand why he was not yet a colonel. Imbued with such a sense of duty, he probably recognised that he had encountered serious difficulties, but was not fit to become a Standartenführer if he did not know how to overcome these difficulties. But this was not enough to make him give up his dream of promotion. He felt that he deserved it.

And then there was Italy, where the results could only be described as disastrous. From this Fascist country, where the race laws had been in force for five years, not one single Jew had been transported. Just the opposite: the German ally had become a hiding place for thousands of Jews from all over central Europe, fleeing from the hunt that he had set in motion.

Italy was definitely a thorn in his side, because it hindered his ascent through the ranks. Now that the Italian Social Republic[6.] had been set up, if he was not able to achieve an impressive success at least there, he would have to wave goodbye to his promotion. And in the SS, those who did not get ahead went backwards!

---

6. *Repubblica Sociale Italiana* – also known as the *Repubblica di Salò*: the puppet Fascist state set up in Nazi-occupied northern and central Italy and led by Benito Mussolini after the Italian government in southern Italy had ratified an armistice with the Allies on the 8 of September 1943. The RSI lasted from the 25th of September 1943 to the 25th of April 1945.

The previous year, at the Wannsee Conference,[7] where they had worked out the Final Solution to the Jewish question, Eichmann had reported that there were 58,000 Jews in Italy. He needed to capture them all – swiftly, efficiently and systematically.

Wishing to make a good start, he decided to begin in the city with the largest number of them and the best conditions for their capture: it still had an old ghetto where many Jews insisted on living, even though more than seventy years had passed since the gates had been pulled down.

It has not been possible to ascertain whether Eichmann attributed a symbolic meaning to the extermination of the Roman Jewish community. The fact that it was the oldest one in Europe did not concern him. They were all "pieces" anyway. Nor did it make much of an impression on him that the Jews had been building their synagogues in Rome for more than two thousand years, since before the birth of Christ. To Eichmann, eradicating that nucleus, so deeply rooted in the city, meant extirpating the deepest root of the "infection" which had spread throughout Europe. Perhaps Eichmann had been told that Roman Jews refused to pass under the Arch of Titus, which stood beside the Colosseum, because of the hatred they felt towards the man who had destroyed the temple in Jerusalem. But that was just folklore: the myths and traditions of his "pieces" were none of his business. There was no room for such reflections in the ordered mind of a transport administrator.

What did occupy his mind was a strong desire for complete

---

7. *Wannsee Conference*: a meeting of senior Nazi officers, held in the Berlin suburb of Wannsee on the 20th of January 1942. The main topic of discussion was a plan for the deportation of the Jewish population of Europe and French North Africa to German-occupied areas in Eastern Europe, where they would be used as slave labour and eventually exterminated.

and resounding success. To sweep away the Jewish "pus" that lodged in Rome – in one fell stroke, like an unstoppable cyclone – would be his most exhilarating mission.

There is no evidence that anyone had ordered him to rush off to Rome to carry out his macabre cleansing. Italy must have been causing other problems for Berlin in the September-October period of 1943, as the Americans were making their way up from the South. But for Eichmann cleaning up Rome, under the Pope's very eyes, was too important. He had to do it despite the misgivings of the German Foreign Ministry on the Wilhelmstrasse. He had to overcome the reluctance of the Wehrmacht, which never willingly supplied the necessary means, with the excuse that they were needed for the war effort (as if eliminating the most poisonous enemies of the Reich would not make victory easier). Yes, this would be the deciding moment of his career.

He was determined to succeed in this ambitious and delicate task, outclassing Kappler[8] who, after the Naples uprising, seemed paralysed by the fear of a revolt that would be even more humiliating in Rome. And a revolt would have broken out if the Romans had defended their Jews, in the same way that the women of Naples had fought the deportation of their young men to Germany.

The successful completion of such an operation, without any consequences or reactions, was to be his masterpiece. It would show them what he was made of and just how good his organisational skills were.

He threw himself body and soul into the task, enlisting

---

8. Herbert Kappler was head of the German police in Rome during World War II, and had the overall responsibility for the deportation of Jews. After the war he was sentenced to life imprisonment in Italy, but was successfully smuggled back to Germany inside a suitcase.

the services of his most clear-headed and expert associate, Captain Theodor Dannecker – a man full of nervous tics, which hid who knows what underlying personality problems.

This time, drawing on his past experience, the Captain would avoid word getting out, as it had done in France. He would take extraordinary measures to ensure success in an environment that was not yet primed for his purpose, due to the fact that its citizens were not hostile to Jews. For the Romans, the people who lived in the ghetto, "li giudii", as they were called in the local dialect, were part of the landscape, like the Colosseum and the dome of St. Peter's. They did not love the Jews, because you can't love people who insist on being different – not just for one generation, but for one hundred – and the Church had been stirring up resentment about them for centuries.

However, this background hostility, which had flared up occasionally in the past, was now countered by the realisation that those people were just poor unfortunate souls, who were like everyone else in every other respect. The Jews were nothing but defenceless fellow sufferers, with problems just like theirs. At the time of the passing of the race laws the overwhelming feeling towards the Jews had been one of solidarity. Respected members of the community continued to be respected. The Romans' vague fondness, as if for distant relatives, was in no way diminished.

Eichmann certainly made sure he was briefed about this widespread feeling, because he left nothing to chance. He made sure that he had all the necessary support from the all-powerful High Command of the SS, in order to overcome any resistance and fear on the part of the diplomats and the army. He showed his order to proceed to both

Kappler and the ambassador to the Holy See. It had been issued by a general of the SS, but Eichmann gave them to understand that it had come from someone even higher up. No one dared stand in his way.

It is very likely that he pressed his superiors for this order, because there was some hesitation in issuing it in Berlin. The departure of many trains from stations all over occupied Europe had still to be organised. Then, if the Pope were to take a clear stance, or if a popular revolt threatened… those two possibilities must have sent shivers down the spines of even the upper echelons of the Reich.

But European trains were a routine matter, and routine was not enough to advance Eichmann's career. What he needed was a resounding success. Rome gave him the perfect chance.

His associate, Dannecker, threw himself into organising the round-up – it had to take everyone by surprise so that all the dreaded complications could be avoided. After the fall of Fascism on the 25th of July, no one had thought to destroy the detailed lists of names and addresses of Roman Jews. An eager Fascist official must have delivered them to him, after removing them from the Ministry of the Interior where they were stored.

With Germanic precision, Dannecker and his men carefully divided Rome into twenty-six Judenaktionsbezirken, all equally balanced according to the number of "pieces" to be taken. An envelope was assigned to each sector and after meticulous checking it was filled with numerous typewritten slips of paper, listing the exact names and addresses of every Jewish family or single person to be taken away. It is hard to visualise over a thousand typed slips of paper set out in order on the tables: the names of the people who would be behind their doors when the SS came violently knocking, to intimidate them or rather, to crush them, as if they had been sent by an angry god, who was implacable and unreachable.

Every member of every family as well as single people: men and women, young and old, boys and girls – whether healthy or sick, rich or poor, demented or sane, educated or illiterate.

Who knows how many hours the Captain's men spent poring over the map of Rome, hunting for those addresses and linking every one of them to the names of its occupants. Then having the slips of paper typed up by Italian clerks and using them to work out the twenty-six numerically balanced zones. Who knows how long they took to estimate how many trucks would be needed to transport all those people, or how much room they deemed would be enough for each adult with one suitcase. And the children? Toddlers under the age of three would have to stay in their parents' arms, but would they also be entitled to a little case? Yes, and so it was necessary to allow a few extra centimetres for that as well. The Captain's men probably discussed and carefully assessed every aspect of the problem.

Another area of concern was the Wehrmacht's reluctance to guarantee the minimum number of vehicles needed to cover all twenty-six zones. "Good God, there's a war on!" the generals kept saying. The Captain also had to fight for men, enough for the necessary companies – keeping in mind that certain operations required specific experience only the SS could provide. In the end, he had to make do with what he was given. He must have been a very capable officer. As history shows, the operation was completely successful, with no complications in the areas it was possible to cover with the available resources.

Finally the plan was ready to put into action – immediately after the Jewish Community of Rome delivered even more than the fifty kilograms of gold they were forced to pay, like a tax to buy the right to survive. It was an amazing demand to make in the middle of the twentieth century. Especially in Rome, where obviously nobody remembered the sword of Brennus and his angry "Vae victis!" ("Woe to the vanquished!").9. The Roman Jews even managed to fool themselves that their right to live had been bought from the Nazis for a few grams of gold per head.

The Captain would have liked to carry out the operation without any Italian help. But it was impossible to make thousands of arrests in an unfamiliar city as big as Rome, at the gates of the Vatican and amongst hostile townspeople, without having to rely on a few locals and interpreters. He tried to keep the number of Roman recruits to an absolute minimum and literally locked them up in the hours immediately preceding the operation, in order to prevent any contact with the outside.

He trusted no one, although he knew that people could be stubbornly optimistic and insist on putting their heads in the sand instead of facing their fears. From his experience elsewhere, he certainly knew that the Jews simply could not imagine what was in store for them. In Rome they were even less inclined to do so, because they had just paid the ransom. That's the way they were, especially in Rome: the flock could see the dome of St. Peter's from their windows and their home had been declared an "open city", even if no one could actually explain what that reassuring label meant.

---

9. *Brennus*: Gaulish leader who occupied Rome in 390 BC. The popular legend says that he forced the people of Rome to ransom their city by paying him a thousand pounds of gold. When they protested, he threw his sword onto the scales, shouting "Vae victis!" (Woe to the vanquished!).

Although plenty of news had filtered through, the Jews were still hopeful. As early as September, people had tried to shake them from their apparently catatonic state in the face of imminent danger. "They asked for gold and we gave it to them. The Germans follow through; when they give their word, they keep it," was their way of thinking.

They say that some snakes hypnotise their prey so as not to miss it when they strike. The same was done by the formal, polite officers who presented themselves at the Community's premises.

In early October, German officers showed up to "view" the texts, some of them thousands of years old, that were kept there. Those ancient documents, which had been respectfully preserved, were not just about Jews; they told the history of Rome, including the first Christian communities formed in the city. They were a cultural treasure that belonged to all humankind. The officers were competent and thorough, examining everything with courtesy and care.

But on the 13th October, two railway wagons appeared in front of the Great Synagogue of Rome, on the boulevard along the Tiber. They had been pulled there along the tram tracks on the "Black Circle Line" that ran around Rome. The next day, still politely but forcefully, they ordered that the precious heritage be loaded into the wagons. This was done by removal men from a cooperative called in to do the job. All the texts were bundled together, with a little extra care taken for fragile scrolls and the most ancient books. All, except for those the removal men threw out of the windows, in the hope that someone would retrieve them and keep them out of the Germans' hands. This did not happen. The optimistic attempt to rescue at least a tiny part of that precious collection was thwarted by bad weather. They were found again months later, after the liberation of Rome. By that time they were almost completely ruined. The man in charge of the Community's assets made fruitless protests to the Germans over the misappropriation. He also sent plaintive letters to the relevant Ministries…

During October there were other signs that should have worried people, but the Jews – still living in their own homes, still decently clothed and fed, like all the other Romans – did not pick them up.

There were increasingly clear hints coming from Northern Europe – especially North-Eastern Europe. There was talk of mass deportations, but even if those awful things were true, everyone was convinced they were only likely to occur in places where that sort of thing could happen. In short, they were tragedies that only affected the Ostjuden, who were used to suffering terrible wrongs that were unheard of in Rome. There were other very tangible warning signs that became increasingly serious. On the day of Kippur a large number of Jews were arrested. People were led to believe it was "because they were anti-Fascist". The unsuspecting Roman Jews fell for it.

On the evening of the 15th of October the laneways of the ghetto rang with Celeste's loud cries.10. She was a Jew who lived in Trastevere, on the other side of the Tiber, opposite the ghetto where the Jews used to be locked up. She had heard from a policeman's wife that all the Jews were going to be arrested, and rushed back to warn her

10. The Celeste of Modiano's narrative is probably based on a real-life person, Celeste Di Porto, mentioned in many historical accounts as a well-known Jewish collaborator with Fascists and Nazis. Celeste Di Porto did attempt to warn the Jews in the Rome ghetto before the round-up of the 16th of October 1943, but also gave a number of them away to the Gestapo for money.

people. She yelled, cried and implored everyone she met to escape that very evening. She was not pleading for help to get away herself, she was urging others to flee. But Celeste was notorious: she was among the most wretched people in the Community. Poor wretches are always predicting new catastrophes, as if bringing them on themselves. They are always afraid of losing what little they have. It was a cruel twist of fate: many members of Celeste's family were known to be insane and her son was more or less thought of as the "village idiot". Who was going to believe the warnings from a social outcast, raving about a highly unlikely mass deportation? In a moment of sheer desperation, the poor woman suddenly tore open her clothes to reveal her bare breasts. If ever proof was needed that what she was saying was the mere product of madness, it was now clear for all to see.

The final warning sign: all through that night in the ghetto, the silence was broken by shots being fired and the noise of bullets hitting the buildings. It was unthinkable that it could have been some drunken soldiers firing into the air for fun. Some things just did not happen in the German army, and if a soldier had been responsible, he would have been arrested immediately. The shooting, on the other hand, went on for a long time.

Captain Dannecker had everything worked out. He wanted to frighten his "pieces", forcing them to stay indoors, holed up and terrified, so that they wouldn't so much as put their noses out of the door in an attempt to escape. Word could have got out and someone might have got away, and then others, and yet more others. The thought that his "pieces" might slip through his fingers just a few hours before their capture was intolerable. The Captain was probably hoping for a promotion, just like his superior.

Celeste, the last herald of doom, had cried out in vain that evening. The SS entered the ghetto in driving rain at 6.30 a.m. on Saturday the 16th of October. They began to bang on doors with the butts of their rifles at the first addresses pulled out of the envelopes for each Judenaktionbezirk.

CHAPTER 6

Early in the morning of Saturday, the 16th of October, there was a loud knocking on the door of Rachel's home. The Germans had come to take her and her parents away. Twenty minutes to get ready and pack some belongings – they could take along money, valuables that weren't too heavy, something to eat and a few clothes. One suitcase each.

Half an hour later, Rachel's father locked the front door, as if the family were going away on a short trip. A journey did in fact await them.

They went down the stairs followed by the bewildered, compassionate looks of some of their neighbours. It was unthinkable that such a close and respectable family could have done anything deserving of punishment, especially the little girl. Her blue eyes, wide open and unflinching, without tears, appealed for help that no one knew how to give and made everyone hang their heads.

A truck was waiting for them not far from the house. The vehicle moved off, slowly and noisily. It went round in circles, its driver lost in a city he didn't know. Eventually it reached the Military Academy in Via della Lungara, next to the Tiber and near the Regina Coeli prison. Keeping close to one another, they entered the large, forbidding building.

There were lots of Jews milling around in the big court-yard: the result of a round-up in the ghetto and the rest of the city, a round-up carried out within a circle drawn on the map of Rome. If the Germans had had more resources on hand that day, the circle would have been wider, the number of Jews in that courtyard bigger. The lack of resources had saved a lot of people, those who lived just outside that circle. But there had been sufficient resources to capture those who were inside it and who hadn't taken notice of the warning signals they had received.

Rachel was inside the circle and along with her, more than a thousand people found themselves in that courtyard. They found comfort in being such a large number: "How could they harm so many people?", "They'll send us off to work. At least we'll get something to eat." And the Germans had confirmed, "We're sending you off to work. Your valuables will come in useful for buying something in the canteen."

Later on, though, they were told to hand over all their possessions: they would be used to provide for the elderly and those who were not going to be able to work. Hope alternated with disappointment as the hours passed; any illusions were quick to disappear. Those thousand people kept ignoring the rumours they must have heard, that their death was the real aim of the Germans, and that it was getting closer.

"It's impossible. What could they possibly gain by killing us?" "They need workers, they're at war." "Anyway, how could they kill thousands of people?" "No, it can't be true, Germans are rational, all that matters to them is the war and winning it. Dead people are no use to anyone."

Rachel was overwhelmed. What crushed her was not so much fear of death or fear of what was to come, but the loss of everything that had surrounded her, that had been her life up until now. She couldn't bear that unbridgeable gap between her past and her present.

"Papà can't defend me or protect me anymore. He can't do anything now…he's no longer 'Papà'."

"Mamma, I'm hungry," she kept saying.

"Here, have this."

She wasn't really hungry; she was just trying to see if her parents were still able to feed her in that courtyard.

"Mamma, I need to go."

"All right, go over there."

"I'm embarrassed. There are other people."

"Don't be embarrassed. They're all women."

At last night came.

"Mamma, I want to go to sleep."

"All right, lie down here. Rest your head on the suitcase. I'll cover you with this."

"But you'll get cold if you give me your coat."

"Don't worry, I'm not cold; I'm going to sit here next to you."

It isn't easy to sleep when a storm is raging round you. Memories chase one another, tumbling over each other; nothing is in its right place any more. There's nothing left to hold on to: home, parents, friends and even the city are no longer the same.

Rachel managed to sleep, although the planned, gradual destruction of identity, set in motion by the Germans in the early hours of that hellish day, had also begun for her and within her.

Her people had been stripped of their homes and possessions, and now were being stripped of their present and their future. They were no longer in control of their own lives. Stripped and subjugated, they were no longer human beings. That Saturday night for the first time, the adults had begun to sense this as they tried and failed to sleep.

And yet those Jews of the Rome ghetto thought that they

had grown a protective shell. They had already experienced the violence of street mobs, stirred up against the killers of Christ whenever any disaster happened. They had already seen the burning and pillaging of their houses, behind the gates of the ghetto. These were houses they couldn't even call their own, because Jews were forbidden to own property – all they were granted was a parody of ownership, something known as the Jus di Gazagà, the right to occupy but not own houses.11. For years, every Sunday, their ears rang with the sermons of a priest who was charged with converting them, or better still, exorcising them. They had already lost some of their children, kidnapped and forcibly baptised, to comfort some barren Christian woman. The Jews of the ghetto had lived through this time and time again, and so were hopeful, despite all. How could things get worse? They weren't frightened by hard labour. They would see the ghetto again...

Sunday passed without their sad situation growing any worse than it had been the day before, except for a humiliating joke: they were made to hand over the keys to their homes, which they had been told to lock carefully before leaving. The keys would allow someone to go there and "get something to eat for everyone". But then no one was given permission to go home. Instead, a few men were sent to buy bread and something to eat with it, using money collected from everyone, whilst their families were held hostage. In the meantime, the keys were being used by the Germans to strip every possession from the Jews' abandoned houses.

---

11. Jus di Gazagà: Gazagà is an Italian adaptation of the Hebrew Hazakah, the Jewish law on the acquisition of property. Modiano refers to a law introduced by Pope Paul IV in 1555, which allowed Italian Jews – forbidden to own properties – to remain in rented properties as long as they wanted to.

Before dawn on Monday the 18th of October, the Jews were ordered to get up and get ready to leave. Rachel wasn't in the first group to move off and had to wait for the second run of the convoy taking them to the train. Through the canvas sides of the truck she caught the occasional glimpse of Rome. She was just able to recognise bits of the city, which she was crossing from side to side for the first time, bound for Tiburtina Station.

"Largo Argentina: I've been here, it's near the Synagogue. I used to come here with Mamma and Papà nearly every Saturday." She recognised the road leading up to Piazza Venezia, but nothing after that as the city became completely unfamiliar.

Cattle trucks were waiting for them. A train made up of about twenty of them stood at the far edge of the station. Nothing surprised Rachel any more. She followed her parents in silence. Hardly any of the others were speaking either. They were made to get into a truck, which closed heavily behind them, plunging them into gloomy semi-darkness. Their eyes quickly adjusted to the dim light and Rachel was able to look around. There were so very many of them packed together, but at least they had room to sit: she could just manage to stretch her legs out in front of her.

The train set off in the early afternoon. It reached Auschwitz Station on the night of Thursday the 21st of October, too late to let its passengers off. It wasn't until dawn the next day that the Germans cleared the trucks. Some people had already died during the journey.

The train had stopped only twice: in Padua and Nuremberg. At Padua they were only given water and in the German city the luckier ones were given some watery broth. Rachel had suffered like everyone else from heat and thirst at the beginning and then from cold at night.

She had complained and cried for herself with resignation rather than anger, and certainly less than others. The adults vented their feelings in other ways: they felt anger and pain at their forced helplessness and on behalf of their children, if they had any.

Along those never-ending rails, Rachel fashioned an invisible shell for herself that dulled her pain. By the end of the journey she was feeling nothing. She had fallen into a sort of trance. She felt she was outside the truck, back in her own world; she recalled her past and imagined her future. This was only a dream; she was going to go back to her room and her life. There was no train, there were no people. Now she was alone. She was travelling along a circle as long as that dream, going round and round, but she would eventually get back to where she had started from. The train was saying this too, she just had to listen: "You.will.go.home – you.will.go.home – you.will.go.home…"

Her expressionless eyes lit up as she heard that message. A shadow of a smile appeared on her lips. It lingered for a long time; every now and again it briefly disappeared and her eyes grew dark. This happened when something bumped against her invisible shell: either the train broke its rhythm or something from outside tried to break in and distract her. Then for a few seconds her fear came back and the wheels said: "You.won't.go.home. – you.won't.go.home – you.won't.go.home."

Luckily this happened less and less frequently as the hours and days went by. At dawn on Friday they got off the train onto a long platform. It was only a stop on the journey round the circle, a journey which was going to be completed at her home, in Rome. Rachel looked around. She saw some strange beings. No one had told her that there were beings like these: bodies like humans and voices like dogs. And they did bark. Some of them were wearing black cloaks, others rags striped like zebras. The ones in cloaks barked, the others were silent.

Nobody looked the new arrivals in the face. The black-cloaked beings didn't even see them. The others avoided their gaze or had no eyes, yet they walked around them, quickly and carefully, focussed on who knows what. Why had nobody ever told her about beings like this, either at home or at school?

"Right, now we have to split up. For a little while, just a little while. A black dog is sorting us out without barking. They've already separated the men from the women, just for a while. I'll see Papà again."

"To the right, to the left, to the right, to the right," a voice rang out.

"Mamma is going to the right; I'm going to the right. That's lucky."

Two lines were being formed. The one on the right was longer, much longer.

"We're going to take a shower. Please God it will be warm."

CHAPTER 7

At the same time, safe in Abruzzo, I was making discoveries great and small. Under different circumstances, it would have been a wonderful holiday.

I watched the wheat being ground in an ancient mill, where a blindfolded donkey laboriously turned the heavy millstone. It walked kilometres every day inside its cramped prison, trudging monotonously round the circle it had worn on the ground. I played at harvesting grapes with the peasants, who did it in earnest and in silence. In September, I pressed the grapes with my bare feet in a vat that was full to the brim and so deep I could have drowned in it. My inexperienced, light feet were given the task of starting the mysterious cycle, ending in a stream of must, which I had the chance to taste for the first time. I picked apples and pears. I sorted them by type and size, which determined what they would be used for. I saw tools being mended, and witnessed the careful ritual of putting them away so that they would be kept in good condition for the following spring. I was there for all the tasks the peasants carried out in autumn, a busy time before the long winter rest.

I also witnessed the cruel tasks, like killing pigs. The ritual slaughter was dreadfully harsh and carried out with cold detachment. This was another discovery: the very same people who had seemed so kind and gentle, were now killing a poor, defenceless creature they had kept for months, almost as though it were a family pet. The poor beast let out desperate, high-pitched shrieks and kicked wildly as the blood spurted into the bowl held under its throat. Not one drop was to be lost. Little by little the victim grew quiet as life left it. The movements of its legs became less frantic, fading to faint, futile twitches.

One pig managed to get away from its butchers as they were slitting its throat. It raced around the yard, letting out piercing squeals. An irregular red trail marked its desperate flight: a splash and a streak, a splash and a streak, corresponding to the wild pumping of its maddened heart. The peasants, both men and women, chased it crossly, cursing because the blood was being wasted.

I would have liked to save its life, to snatch it away from those merciless hands. I was tempted to run towards it, as if by catching it in my arms I could have spared it from death. I knew it was crazy to even think of it. I had also learnt that the lives of the villagers depended on those sacrifices, and I realised that I too would eat it. But if it could have made any difference to the pig's survival, I would have been willing to give up my share.

At least it should have been spared from torture. They threw boiling water over the pig while it was still alive. The first time I saw this I found the strength to protest, and shouted desperately, "Can't you wait till it's dead?" They laughed at me for being soft and only one of those present thought my objection worthy of an explanation, "While the pig is still alive it's easier to pull out the bristles because of the way scalded skin reacts." Then death came at last. Since then I have come across other people who have seen that kind of killing. Like me, none of them have ever been able to forget it.

There followed swift and professional, almost surgical, operations in which the carcass could be quartered, chopped up and cured without any waste. Chops, hams, blood for black puddings and intestines, which were used as casings for sausages: all edible stuff which, appropriately rationed, would last for a whole year. "Waste not, want not," they taught me. This stopped me from judging them too harshly, because I was going to eat it too. I was no better than they were.

But life there also had its mellow moments, though tinged with sadness, the way autumn evenings in the country are. As when it got dark and the fire was being lit, while outside it was raining and the cold was already making itself felt. Or at dinnertime, sitting at a wooden tabletop on which steaming polenta was spread an inch thick, before a tomato sauce or hot melted lard with bits of crackling was poured over it.

Everyone used their forks on that yellow expanse splattered with sauce, marking out the little piece they were about to eat; then the next piece and the next again. Children were allowed to carve out irregular shapes, securing one or two more sauce-covered pieces. But we could only trespass so far: we too had to abide by an unspoken code of ethics that demanded respect for the other diners. That shared table was where I first learnt the rules of social interaction. It taught me that the rights of every person are limited by those of their neighbours, that there is always someone with whom we must share what is available. From that polenta-covered tabletop, I absorbed a culture that was totally different from the selfish culture where everyone eats from an individual plate. Throughout my life few words have been as effective in conveying respect for the rights of others.

Our little corner of Italy seemed at peace that autumn. I would remember those days as happy, if they had not been spoiled by the constant anxiety at not hearing any news of my family. Nobody came from Rome, and so Guido and I were in the dark about the fate of all of our relatives. During the day, I managed not to think about it, but at night it was impossible, especially after dinner and before we went to sleep. Sometimes homesickness and worry were so strong that I burst into tears.

Once Guido made a careless slip. In Civitatomassa we were in no real danger of being recognised as Jews. It's probable that its inhabitants didn't even know that we existed. And yet, Guido managed to create a dangerous situation with the one person who *was* aware of the existence of Jews.

Not long after our arrival, one evening we were playing in front of the village church when the priest arrived from Scoppito – the closest town to Civitatomassa – to celebrate mass, as he did every Sunday. Instead of sneaking away, we stayed with the other kids and, being curious, went into the church with them. Naturally, the priest noticed the new faces and asked us who we were and where we came from. When he heard we were from Rome, he asked us about our schooling. Without even thinking, Guido answered that he'd completed third-year high school. The priest's face lit up as if touched by divine grace: the boy standing before him had been sent by the Lord – he could never have hoped for a more suitable altar boy. Not only could he read, he'd also studied Latin!

Guido and I exchanged terrified looks, and then he muttered some pathetic excuse, such as "I wouldn't be any good at it." The poor priest, without a second thought for details, enthusiastically reassured him and started making all sorts of plans for future masses.

We ran to Lanzi and asked him to sort things out, but intelligent and shrewd as he was, he couldn't work miracles. He could never explain to the priest why his plans couldn't be carried out. Each Sunday from then on (and there were more than a few), he was forced to make ever more improbable excuses to explain why we hadn't gone to mass. In the end he resorted to saying that we city boys were used to sleeping in. Every time we saw Lanzi coming back from church, we felt guiltier and guiltier. We could imagine the priest lecturing him on not being a good Christian and not setting a good example.

War is not something you can put out of your mind... Two or three times we found ourselves face to face with Allied pilots who had been shot down and were trying to join the Resistance fighters in the mountains. These meetings threw me into a state of unhappy frustration. I would have liked to tell them everything, give them some practical help, be their guide, do something useful, but I couldn't. I was too young and I wasn't familiar with the area around the village. Once we met two soldiers. One asked Guido, "Dove possible ... transversare main road ...less danger Germans, Deutsch?" From where we were, we could just see a bit of the main road. But where could we take them to? Which would be the least dangerous place for them to cross? Like me, Guido felt crushed by the weight of responsibility. We couldn't give them an answer, only a helpless, apologetic look as they went on their way.

It was the terrifying thought of making a mistake that might have been fatal for them, rather than fear of giving ourselves away that held us back. We knew that the villagers regularly helped airmen who had been shot down. They would hide them for a few days and then guide them into the mountains to join the Resistance fighters. One day there were eight of them hidden in a barn (there had never been so many at once) when two German trucks started coming up the steep slope to the village. Panic spread like wildfire. In a flash, all the windows were pulled shut by trembling hands. All the men disappeared and we children were snatched from our games in the street and taken inside.

The fear caused by the unexpected visit quickly dissipated: the Germans had come to buy a couple of cows from a villager, who had offered to sell them a few days earlier. For the record, they didn't end up buying them, because the animals showed signs of tuberculosis. The Germans got back into their trucks, annoyed that they'd had a wasted trip. Backing out down the street to the main road, they grazed the wall of the barn for the second time. Inside, I imagine, the eight men were levelling their handguns, ready to fight to the last man. That skeleton crew from a poorly armed German supply unit would have been no match for them, but by the following day, there would have been nothing left of Civitatomassa and its inhabitants but a memory. It was the closest I ever got to seeing armed combat, and all I could have done was watch. But in my childish imagination, I would have liked to be a part of it.

And that's the way things continued to be: always led by the hand, always a bystander with no control whatsoever over the things that happened to me. I was old enough to understand what was going on around me, but not old enough to take part in it.

CHAPTER 8

The fireplace was the only source of warmth in the houses and the only means of cooking food. Women learned early how to juggle the distance from the flames, the heat of the fire and the cooking times so that everything was ready (neither burnt nor raw, neither undercooked nor overcooked) when the family sat down to eat. Polenta or pasta, potatoes or beans, meat or vegetables, each had their own cooking time and all were cooked on that single fire. In the afternoon, the dance of the pans started in the wide fireplace: high heat, low heat, coals, closer to the flames, further from the flames, pans hanging high over the fire or almost touching it…

One evening in mid-December we were all indoors. Due to the cold and early nightfall, our brief adventures outside were finished for the day. We were warming ourselves in front of the fire, whilst Mamma Lanzi was juggling her pans. Suddenly we heard a voice from the street, "Guido! Guido Modiano!"

Instinctively, my brother moved towards the window, but Lanzi caught him by the arm, and pulled him back.

"Stay where you are. I'll see who's looking for you."

He stuck his head out, "Oh, it's you, Mancinelli. What are you doing here?"

"I've come to fetch the boys. Their father sent me."

"Come on up and we'll talk about it."

Neither my brother nor I had ever met Mancinelli, but Lanzi knew him because he was the painter my father hired for jobs in the buildings he managed. He had really come to fetch us. We learned from him that the Americans had got as far as Cassino, barely a hundred kilometres from Rome. No one could imagine that the American front would be stuck there for very long. Worried that we might be cut off from Rome by the shifting front line, my father had decided to send for us. Mancinelli had four children and travelling in those days was dangerous, even without two Jews tagging along. Despite that, he had taken on the job, and certainly not for the promise of payment.

We had been in Civitatomassa for three months and that was my first really peaceful evening. I'd had a great time there, but every day and every evening were tainted with worry about what was happening to my mother, father and Elena.

"They're all fine," Mancinelli quickly let us know.

"They're all fine, I'm so happy! And tomorrow I'll see them again!" A nightmare was coming to an end, and I felt a sense of freedom and calm that I hadn't felt for a long time. That was how I saw things at that moment, when I was unaware of the impact reality would have on my dream. Rome was still a long way from being liberated and things had not gone all that well for my family.

I was happy but reproached myself for feeling like that: I thought I was being ungrateful to the Lanzis because I was so glad to be leaving. It wasn't as if I had any complaints or as if I hadn't been treated well in their house! I was afraid that my joy might be visible and made an effort to contain it, for fear of being mis-understood, but restraining it was really hard. I think that even the rabbit, if it had still been alive, would have noticed it.

"If Papà has sent for us," I thought, "it means that soon, very soon, we'll all be together again in our own home."

Even Mancinelli was convinced that the Americans would soon arrive in Rome. He brought some news-papers with him. I had never paid them any attention before, but I missed them through all those days when we were so cut off. The world was in deep turmoil in the winter of '43 and only tiny fragments of news reached us, reported by a villager, who heard it from someone, who in turn had heard it from someone else, and so on.

The Lanzis also seemed to be happy when the mes-senger arrived from Rome, all except for Gabriele, who was about to lose his playmates. To celebrate, that evening Signora Lanzi made tagliatelle, using one egg per person and with a special sauce. I could never have imagined just how much I would yearn for that hearty meal in the not too distant future. Over dinner, Mancinelli told us about his eventful journey, which ended with a lift from a German truck to the foot of the hill where the village perches.

"I made an arrangement with the soldier to come back and pick us up tonight – at three in the morning, because he has to drive back to Rieti. From there it won't be hard to get to Fara Sabina and then, to Rome. All going well, by this time tomorrow we'll be home."

It sounded like an excellent plan that would also be fun, with a ride on a military truck – though it wasn't up to me to say yes or no. I hardly slept a wink that night, but when they called me just after two in the morning, I leapt out of bed as if I'd been there for a solid twelve hours.

We were on the main road at the agreed spot in plenty of time before the appointment, but the German didn't show up. We waited in vain for hours. Private traffic was non-existent and very few military vehicles were on the road that night. It was well after daybreak when a German truck finally stopped for us. Before letting us get in, the driver bargained with Mancinelli over the price of a ride as far as Rieti. Once on board, we realised that the soldier had a good nose for business, because we weren't his only passengers: he picked up others along the way, more than got off. In a short time there were a lot of us on that makeshift means of transport, which was not designed for passengers and didn't have any seats.

After an endless wait in the freezing dark of December, the truck moved off. So ended my first (almost) sleepless night, spent walking up and down the road to warm my feet. I was in my good shoes again, with their "autarkic" soles (which was how we described shoddy goods made in Italy). The cold had moved up my legs, which were bare to my thighs, and penetrated my whole body.

These days the first leg of our journey would be considered short, but back then it wasn't. In any case, it was long enough to give us more than one shock. We had hardly gone any distance at all, when a plane started circling above our heads, constantly changing altitude and distance, the noise of the engine getting louder, then softer. The uneven speed of the truck reflected the driver's fears: fast for a stretch, then slow, then fast again; a stop in a sheltered spot and then away again. In the back, concealed by the tarpaulins that blocked any view of the outside, we silently endured the erratic driving, using our ears to try and gauge just how much danger we were in. A couple of old peasant women recited prayers under their breath.

The pilot of the plane must have been after more glorious targets than a truck that day; perhaps that was why he didn't waste one single volley of machine-gun fire on us. Finally he flew off as quickly as he had borne down on us.

The reprieve didn't last long. On the approach to Antrodoco, the road plunged into the township in a series of hairpin bends. From the top of the hill, someone realised that we were again heading into a dangerous situation, just as bad as the previous one. Moving aside the tarpaulin that hid us, they had seen the Germans rounding people up.

We were already on one of their trucks and the men knew it would be easy for the driver to make them change vehicles. I realised it, too, when Mancinelli pulled some money out of his pocket and gave it to Guido. "If they take me, go to Rieti, to the bus station, and try and get on a bus to Fara Sabina. From there, get another bus or the train to Rome. Look after him," he said, pointing to me. "This should be enough."

I looked at Guido to see how frightened I should be. He was dumbfounded and nodded as Mancinelli gave him more instructions: what we should say to ask for help, whom and what to avoid …

Everyone held their breath. The truck, in the meantime, entered the village and slowed down. The driver had principles when it came to business (in any case, he would have had difficulty explaining the presence of civilians on board his truck) and stuck to his side of the bargain. Easing past his fellow soldiers, he took us to the agreed drop-off point. Through small gaps between the tarpaulins, we peeked out at what was going on. We could hear the curt orders of the German hunters, the heavy sounds of their boots and the breathless gasps of their prey running down the narrow alleys of their village. Their familiarity with the area was their only advantage in the uneven fight. But I'm afraid that very few managed to evade capture that day.

In Rieti, we managed to have a quick bite to eat in a *trattoria* before rushing to buy tickets for the bus to Fara Sabina. There was already a long queue of people shouting. I was left to look after our suitcases. I did this with such care that I fell asleep on top of them, overcome by tiredness after my plate of steaming soup and the warmth of the weak sun mercifully shining above us.

Our bus arrived at around two in the afternoon. Even for those days it was old, and it wheezed and shuddered every time the motor turned over. It was like an annoyed cat shaking the water off its back after coming through a puddle. Its colour, by then barely recognisable, must have once been blue. The long muzzle in front of the passenger compartment, with its coat of loose metal panels, conveyed its exhaustion and foretold its imminent demise. We weren't successful in the race to grab seats – all we got was standing room on the rear platform. However, I managed to win and defend a relatively privileged position. I was squashed with my face pressed against the large rear window and I could see the scenery – even though it was only views of the countryside I was leaving behind, not the places I was going towards. Of course, I would have been happier sitting next to the driver, but I was pretty happy anyway. I knew that I could never have got to sit in that seat: too many people wanted to get on, all of them were bigger than me and not prepared to move aside for a child.

When the bus finally left Rieti, everything ran smoothly for a while – if that is how you can describe a journey in which every time the bus accelerated the mass of people standing behind lurched into me, squashing all the air out of my lungs. Each time it slowed down I managed to fill my lungs and breathe. I was having fun watching the road disappear behind us. All of a sudden, I saw a large black object rolling quickly down it. I just had time to wonder, "What on earth could that be?" before hearing shouts and feeling painful jolts to my body. I was unaware of what had happened and long moments went by, during which my main emotion was amused curiosity rather than the fear I should have been feeling.

Eventually we came to a halt. The bus was listing to one side, tilted towards the steep shoulder of the road. Very cautiously, we started to get off. The rear axle had snapped and the object I had seen running away from under our feet was a right-hand rear wheel. With one wheel missing, the driver had cleverly managed to keep the heavy vehicle on the road and bring it to rest, leaning to one side. But now it stood sideways, completely blocking the road. The rear of the bus was hanging over the edge of the embankment. Its engine continued conscientiously to turn over, but its frame had had it. Life was running out for the old bus.

We were all in a state of excitement and had to stretch our legs, if only to take a walk around the wounded beast. There was an urge to talk about what had happened, to relieve the tension. Everyone commented upon our lucky escape. I must have shared that feeling too, otherwise I would never have had the courage to tell the others what I had seen from my little corner. For a few moments everyone was willing to listen to what I had to say.

Then gradually an awareness of our predicament replaced our elation. We realised a way had to be found of getting another bus to us. Not an easy thing to do – the nearest town was a few kilometres away and there were no vehicles on the road. The wait risked being a long one. When would they notice that we hadn't arrived? We grew more uneasy as time went by.

Daylight was beginning to fade when a German convoy appeared ahead of us.

"What are they doing? Why are they stopping?"

The Germans had in fact stopped, and it looked as if they were reluctant to proceed. After a few minutes, and with much caution, the convoy started moving again. The soldiers came closer, levelling their weapons at us. They looked us over, full of suspicion, before concluding that these unarmed, shabbily dressed civilians waving them on were not Resistance fighters trying to ambush them. The bus blocking the road was not a clever trap.

They reached us at last but couldn't get past, as they didn't have a vehicle which could push the carcass off the road. The Germans were annoyed at their travel schedule being disrupted, and we were disappointed because they were no use to us. Luckily, they were impatient to move on (all soldiers worship schedules) and took control of the situation, in their own way. Cautiously, but firmly, they made the Italians push the bus carcass until a part of the road was cleared – just enough for one of their cars to pass, with two wheels on the roadway and two on the steep shoulder running alongside it. The slope was so steep that for a moment I was afraid the car might roll over; but to everyone's relief, it got past and sped off towards the faraway point from where we had come.

By now it was quite dark and we could do nothing but wait. There was still the problem of clearing the road. The rest of the convoy was still stuck and no rescue vehicle would be able to get past the body of the bus lying across the road.

Some of the passengers tried in vain to persuade the German officer in charge to ask for help on our behalf in Fara Sabina, our destination. The officer didn't even listen, and even worse than that, insisted that we Italians should shift the bus. Our people had to give in and obey even though they were afraid: the bus was unsteady and every time they pushed, it threatened to roll on top of them. The Germans, who were many, younger and armed, stood by and seemed to enjoy watching the Italians straining to get the bus pointing in the right direction and eventually succeeding.

After another two hours we reached Fara Sabina. It was already night and no buses or trains would be leaving for Rome until the next morning. Because of the curfew nothing was open and nothing was stirring anywhere. In those days, all life came to a halt at night. We had no choice but to go to the station and resigned ourselves to spending the night in the cold waiting room, under the feeble light of a single bulb. Another night to get through, longer and much more uncomfortable than the previous one, some of which I had at least been able to spend in bed. Long hours lay ahead of us fighting the cold, which managed to be more punishing than lack of sleep. Within me, an unpleasant duel played out between those two needs, one or the other gaining the upper hand as the night progressed.

At dawn, Mancinelli went to try and find a cup of milk and a little bread – especially for me, because I was clearly exhausted. He thought he had plenty of time, because the next train for Rome wasn't supposed to leave until late morning. A few moments later he ran back, panting, and pulled me up from the bench where I was fighting for a few more minutes' sleep, as Guido was doing on another bench.

"Come on, quick! We're leaving on that hospital train."

I turned round, and through the glass door to the platform and tracks I saw a little convoy of electric railcars that had silently pulled into the station. It was a hospital convoy. I don't know how, but Mancinelli had managed to talk the engine driver into letting us ride with him. In a rush and still starving, we clambered up into his amazing cab to find that we were not his only guests. I was bursting with excitement: leaving in an electric locomotive was beyond my wildest dreams. The train set off almost at once. The tiny cab had just enough room for the seven or eight passengers it was carrying. I was put into a small space next to a metal wheel that I think operated the handbrake.

The silence produced by our arrival was soon broken. The tightness of the space encouraged conversation, and the passengers and the two railwaymen on duty started talking again. They were discussing the situation in general, the war, the scarcity of food, and the Germans. They sounded surprisingly critical. Even a man who was wearing the uniform of the Fascist militia used language that his superiors, if they had wanted to play it down, would have described as defeatist; if not, they would have had to call him a traitor. As on the outbound one before it, this train journey provided me with a range of people's opinions. Born under Fascism, I had never heard anyone talk openly about what they thought. Hearing people speak this freely surprised me so much that I felt frightened, as if their outspokenness might eventually turn against me.

Mancinelli spoke less than the others, because he was afraid of undercover provocateurs. But he couldn't remain entirely aloof either: that might have made *him* look like a spy. So he used words strategically, nodding and agreeing every now and again, or offering a comment when he felt that people were watching him. My attention flitted back and forth from the tracks rushing towards me to the conversations going on around me, wavering between the hypnotic sound of the train as it slid along the rails and the thrill of hearing those frank, unexpected words.

A little before eight, the train came to the outskirts of Rome. It stopped for the few seconds it took to let us three get off. The engine was already moving again as they threw us our cases. We trudged up a country lane. When we got to the top, we were in Via Nomentana, the road where Mancinelli lived, near the city centre.

A refreshment kiosk was open and at last I was able to put something warm in my stomach. Then a bus took us the rest of the way to Mancinelli's house. We got there more than thirty hours after we had set out from our refuge in Abruzzo. It had been an exceptionally rough journey, even for those times. We had travelled little more than a hundred kilometres.

CHAPTER 9

Once again we were in a house with running water and a toilet: back to luxury!

I slept through the first of what turned out to be several days in our comfortable haven. Our worries weren't over – just the opposite. There was no sign of my parents and Mancinelli didn't know how to get in touch with them; he didn't know their whereabouts, for obvious reasons.

In addition to that, on one of those evenings, a *repubblichino* (which is how we disparagingly referred to the militiamen of Mussolini's Republic of Salò) had knifed Mancinelli's eldest son. They hadn't fought over politics and the wound in his side wasn't serious (they quickly realised that it could just be treated by a friend who was a medical student), but such a violent incident made our hosts anxious and scared. What if the militiaman tried to finish off what he'd started? Even though no one spelled it out for us, our presence complicated things.

I was in the bathroom on the morning of the fourth day, when suddenly the door opened and my mother appeared. Overcome by emotion, she ran in and gave me a hug. I hugged her back with only one hand, because I still had a piece of paper in the other...

The three previous days had been lost due to a

misunderstanding. My parents had gone to wait for us at the bus station every evening, because that's where they expected us to arrive, whereas Mancinelli thought they would turn up at his place, once we had missed the bus on the day we were meant to leave. That morning, my mother, sick with worry, had found the courage to go and see Signora Mancinelli to ask if she had any news. Since we hadn't shown up, she hoped that we had been held up in Abruzzo and hadn't imagined finding us at the Mancinellis'. She was especially worried that she might face a distraught woman accusing my mother of getting her husband arrested, or, at the very least, of jeopardising his life by asking him to fetch two Jewish boys.

Guido and I were moved from the Mancinellis' home to another one. We went to stay with Mario's family – I don't think I ever knew his surname. He had been the chauffeur for my mother's family, until the Great Depression of 1929 had drastically reduced the circumstances of my grandfather and Uncle Alberto, who were both stockbrokers. Mario had a deep scar on one eyebrow from a serious car accident many years before, but this did not disfigure his honest face. He had lost sensation in the region of the scar, but I wasn't to know that. He would sit me on his knee and press hard against the numb spot with the points of a fork. I couldn't believe that it didn't hurt and would shout at him to stop, while trying to wrest the fork from his hands. He would laugh at how gullible I was, but I let him repeat the game and tried to pull the fork away again and again.

Mario and his wife, like all the others, accepted the risky job of looking after us. If they had been found out, the head of the family would have been deported and his death would very probably have followed. We stayed with them for a week, cocooned in the warm, almost playful atmosphere of a home where a stream of friends came and went in a constant flow.

Some of them didn't seem to be making cheerful social calls though, and took Mario aside for a quiet talk. Later on, I found out for certain that Mario was part of the Resistance: I think Papà knew this and consequently took us away from there as soon as possible.

It was close to Christmas when my living arrangements changed again, for the fifth time in three months. Guido, as I found out later, went to live with my parents. They were no longer sticking quite so closely to the safety rule of living apart, without any family member knowing the whereabouts of the others. Perhaps my father was deluding himself that the Americans were about to liberate Rome, but more likely he was running out of people he could ask to hide us.

As early as October, my mother had left her hiding place in the nursing home on the outskirts of Rome and gone back to live with my father. Now, Guido was going to join them. My sister, who had been staying in the countryside near Viterbo, was now living with a lady who was over ninety years old: the terrible Signora Penelope, whom I would eventually meet.

My new refuge was the Crespis' apartment. Arnaldo Crespi was a fat man: his chubby, round face and ample girth were the fleshy expression of his generous nature. He had gone to university with my father and they had remained firm friends over the years, even though their lives had taken different paths. Having me to stay under those circumstances was great proof of that friendship. The Crespis had three boys and another child on the way. Since I had already turned seven, I fitted in between the older two and the youngest.

It was Christmas. If things had been normal, it would have been the best time to be their guest, because of the parties, tombolas and other family games.[12] But things weren't normal and parties were in no way compatible with my situation as a stowaway. The family entertained friends nearly every day, one of whom was the caretaker's daughter who often came to play with the Crespi boys. Unfortunately, all caretakers were bound by a police order to report any new tenant, including children – even a nephew evacuated from the South, which was how they introduced me.

The order left no doubt, and after a couple of enjoyable afternoons, the Crespis were obliged to say that I would be leaving the next day. From that moment on, my prison was one of the bedrooms, where I ran every time anyone rang the doorbell. And there I would stay until the intruder had gone. During those holidays there were lots of intruders. Their games dragged on for whole afternoons, which I spent alone in silence and darkness. Yes, darkness, because in those days no one would have left a light on in an empty room. Unluckily for me, the bedroom doors had frosted glass panels which showed if a light was on – a waste which never went unnoticed by the visitors.

A whole afternoon was a long time to go without visiting a bathroom, especially for a child. We hadn't foreseen this the first time I went to hide and nobody

12. *Tombola*: a game similar to Bingo, with numbers from 1 to 90, still very popular in Italy.

closed the door to the dining room, where the guests were. To get to the bathroom, I had to cross the passageway into which the dining room opened, with the risk of being seen. But luck, which is on the side of the bold, came to my aid and nobody noticed the shadow dashing by, first in one direction, then the other, like a fleeting ghost. After that, the door was scrupulously kept shut "to keep the room warm".

Sooner or later though, even the cleverest stowaways run into trouble along the way. One day someone rang the doorbell and I hurried into one of the safe rooms. It was the caretaker's daughter. Each of the Crespis probably thought that one of the others was keeping an eye on her, but that wasn't the case. The girl was left alone and became impatient. She started looking for the boys and came into the room where I was. This time the frosted glass in the door helped me: I saw the shape of the girl on the other side and I just had time to dive under the bed.

By now, everyone realised what was going on and rushed into the room, which quickly filled up with all the members of the family. I saw them searching with their eyes, trying to locate me. Signora Crespi was the first to guess where I was hiding. She motioned to me with her hand and I made myself less visible. I had stuck my head out a bit, to show them how clever I'd been, thus running the risk of spoiling my previous smart move. It would have been difficult enough to explain why I was still around, let alone what I was doing under the bed!

To give me a break from my life in hiding, as well as a little fresh air, every now and again Signor Crespi took me out with his own children. The caretaker might have seen me as I slipped past her little lodge, surrounded by the Crespi boys, but we decided to risk it. We discovered that after lunch the woman left her post and agreed, if she ever spotted me, to say that I had come back to visit "that very morning" and I would be gone by evening. We could only have used the excuse once, then I wouldn't have been able to go out again for a very long time, until the fib became plausible again. Luckily, the dreaded event never happened, and every now and then I got a breath of fresh air – no more than once every ten to fifteen days, though.

One afternoon, during one of our outings, we walked into a trap: the Germans had set up road blocks on all the streets around us. They closed the circle in a flash and set about methodically checking the papers of everyone within the area the soldiers had surrounded. The Germans were calm, almost peaceful, and didn't look as if they were after anyone in particular. Obviously, this was one of the routine round-ups that they carried out from time to time in various areas of the city.

I tried to act like any little boy, casually curious about the soldiers, but I could only stare straight ahead, unable to turn my eyes towards the German. I should have been looking at him with admiration, but only managed a surreptitious glance to check what he was doing. In short I would say that I definitely looked guilty; if it hadn't been for my age I'm sure I would have attracted the soldier's attention.

That day I learned what it was like to be caught in a trap: I experienced simultaneously panic, resignation, fury and the hope of somehow escaping. These emotions knotted together, creating a tangle I couldn't unravel, a lump which took my breath away, as if the air couldn't get to my lungs. I knew that the show of force wasn't meant for me, but fear doesn't listen to logic – it keeps it at bay. As we filed past, the Germans may well have heard my heart beating wildly. But no one took any notice of a fat man who was going home with four little boys holding onto him, two on each hand. The soldiers, armed to the teeth, didn't pay much attention to us, and after a half-hearted look at Crespi's ID sent us on our way with a barely discernible movement of their machine guns.

The little fish had slipped through their net, but had seen with his own eyes how easily the net could close around him at any time. I had a few more scares. One day I was on a tram with my father, who was taking me back to the Crespis'. I had moved away from him to go and stand near the driver. I was familiar with the route and knew at which stop we had to get off. One stop before, I went back to rejoin Papà. The tram was unusually empty. I walked its entire length without seeing my father. I turned around and walked back, but still couldn't see him. The thought tore through my mind like lightning: "They've taken him, and he didn't call out so that I wouldn't be taken, too." Once again, I desperately went up and down the tram from one end to the other.

"I'm right, I'm right. He's not on the tram…they've taken him."

I knew it was a mistake, but I couldn't help myself: I burst into loud, uncontrollable sobs. From behind a newspaper, the shocked face of my father came into sight. That damned paper gave me the biggest fright of my life. The other passengers were looking at me in amazement; I felt that I needed to give them some sort of explanation.

"I thought that you'd got off," I said to my father. It was a plausible excuse for my crying, which I was still struggling to control.

I felt ridiculous, but I didn't really care: Papà was right there with me and he understood what I had been afraid of, but he couldn't show it. He laid a hand on my shoulder and gave it a comradely squeeze. That was the first moment of adult understanding he and I shared.

CHAPTER 10

Once or twice a week my parents came to see me. It was wonderful when they arrived, and hell when they left. Despite all my brave resolutions, I just wasn't able to let them leave without bursting into tears. I wasn't being difficult; I knew that I might never see them again. Guido was always with them. After a few of their visits I put him on the spot, and he admitted what I had suspected for quite a while: he had gone to live with them.

Why hadn't I been allowed to? Why did I have to be on my own, cooped up in the home of strangers? I found this unbearably unfair, even though I had nothing against the people who were looking after me and who tried so hard to comfort and cheer me up every time my parents left. I did appreciate their efforts, but saying goodbye to my parents was still too high a price to pay.

During one of their early visits, I asked where Uncle Alberto was and why he hadn't yet come to see me. I was expecting them to answer that he was out of Rome. My father gave a start, Guido's body stiffened and my mother's face contracted into a grimace, as tears welled up behind her glasses.

"He'll come one of these days, hopefully," someone

replied, not very convincingly. I kept on asking questions about him – I was frightened because I sensed something wasn't right. I wanted to be told the truth. I think someone eventually said the word "arrested". I knew at once that I would never see him again. "The Germans are taking the Jews," the words echoed loudly in my head. Uncle Alberto was my idol. Everybody said I took after him, which set me apart from Guido and Elena, and made me happy. My uncle had never married and adored the children of his only and beloved little sister, my mother. I was certain that I was his favourite and was proud of it. Since I was the littlest (the *piccolo*), he had nicknamed me, "Count Piccolomini", a reference to a noble Roman family. I could sense the affection behind the name and what's more, he hadn't given any nicknames to either my brother or sister.

Nearly every one of the very few toys I ever received were gifts from him and the first record I ever listened to was played on an enormous wooden gramophone that he had given us. He hadn't been to see me yet because he could no longer come! Why hadn't it dawned on me earlier, when he hadn't been there on the day we came back to Rome! If he'd been able to, he would have turned up to greet me! I would never ever see him again: not for a single moment did I hope he would return. Sadly I wasn't wrong. Only my mother continued to hope against all hope. "He speaks German," she would say, "Perhaps they'll use him as an interpreter."

I was scared by how easily my mother could delude herself and stunned that, young as I was, I could see more clearly than she just how things stood. How could it be that I was more of a realist than my mother? I had grasped the fact that in order to kill people it isn't necessary to talk to them: those who mean to kill have no use for interpreters.

By then, I knew what came next after "they're taking the Jews." We all knew it, except for my mother who didn't want to believe it.

Uncle Alberto had fought in World War I. He'd been wounded at Bligny and had been awarded a silver medal. At the end of the war he was demobbed with the rank of captain. So, when the Germans occupied Rome he decided to try and enlist in Badoglio's army.[13.] One day in early November he went to lunch at my parents'. Sitting at the table, he announced, "There's a chance that I'll try to cross the front line tomorrow with a group of men on the run, but it will be really difficult this time, because I only found out about it yesterday. It might be too late. If it's not, we'll go to Fiumicino and from there by fishing boat to Naples."

Neither my father nor my mother tried to talk him out of it. "Be careful," was all they said, "Let us know if you don't go."

He only revealed his plans just before it was time to leave. He didn't want my parents to spend the whole meal torn between the desire to hold him back from the dangers of such a risky undertaking, and the fear of cutting him off from a way of escape. On the stairs as he was leaving, to allay the anxiety he had created he

---

13. *Badoglio*: fascist military commander in the Ethiopian war, appointed Prime Minister of Italy by the King after Mussolini was deposed on the 25th of July 1943. Together with the King, he fled Rome on the 9th of September and was Head of the Italian government backed by the Allies in Southern Italy.

said goodbye with a predictable "Don't worry!" and an unpredictable "Eia, eia Alalà!" My parents said their goodbyes with a forced smile.

The meaningless words of that Fascist war cry were the last they heard him say. In our minds, my uncle died mocking his executioners. But it is very little comfort.

He did manage to leave at dawn the next day. It was a journey organised by an informer – someone called Scarpato – who was paid five thousand lire for every person arrested. The Germans decided whether or not to stop each truck, or fishing boat. If it carried black marketeers, small-time crooks, or people who didn't matter, the journey went ahead, giving credibility to the informer. But if the passengers were worth catching, the Germans stepped in. That day, Badoglio's nephews were in the group, making it a very nice catch for the SS. The truck was stopped in front of the Pyramid of Cestius, at the start of Via Ostiense, and the passengers arrested. For as long as she could, my mother used a false name and took packages of essential food items and a few personal effects to my uncle, who was in the Regina Coeli prison.

In January, Uncle Alberto was still in prison. My father found out that a Captain Mayer, whom he had known as a civilian before the war, was stationed with the SS. One morning he took Guido with him to their headquarters at the Hotel Flora and asked to speak to the captain. They made my father fill out a form with his personal details. To avoid being picked up on the spot, Papà changed his first name from Saul to Paolo. Then he sat down in the waiting room, expecting to be either called in or taken away. He didn't have to wait long. An adjutant summoned him and the captain received him with embarrassed kindness. What follows is the exchange that took place between the two men, just as my father told it to us.

"Do you realise how reckless you've been? I should arrest you."

"I came to see the Mr Mayer I knew in the past and I'm addressing the man I knew then."

The officer then asked him the reason for his visit, even though I imagine he had already guessed it.

"I've come about my brother-in-law who is in Regina Coeli." He told Mayer my uncle's name, Alberto Chimichi.

The captain pressed a buzzer. A soldier appeared and the Captain gave him an order. A few moments later, he reappeared carrying a folder.

"He was trying to cross the front line in order to fight against us."

"He's being hunted here and tried to escape – he's only human."

"Yes, but that's not the problem. The fact is that your brother-in-law is Jewish, and I have no power over the matter. I have no power when it comes to the enforcement of the race laws. I'm sorry."

It was true. They said goodbye to each other, expressing the hope that circumstances would be different next time they met. Predictably, my father did not achieve anything, but at least he and my brother got out of there alive.

In early February, my mother went to the prison to take her brother his usual package of food and clean laundry.

"He's been transferred," she was told by a prison guard.

"Where to?"

"We don't know."

My mother tried to find out more but her questions were left unanswered.

A few months after the liberation of Rome we received two cards from Uncle Alberto, via the Red Cross. He had sent them from the internment camp in Fossoli, near Modena in northern Italy.

One was dated late March and the other the 4th of April. The latter ended with the words, "I'm well. We are leaving tomorrow, destination unknown."

After that, nothing. My mother tried unsuccessfully to find out what had happened to him. Once the war was over, she kept showing photographs of my uncle to the death camp survivors, who streamed through Rome for months. I don't know how many of them she met. She wanted to know at least where he had died.

"Have you seen him? Do you recognise him?" she asked them all, showing the photos. No one had seen him. I can remember the expression on those survivors' faces. They barely glanced at the photos – just enough to show they'd looked. Then they turned to my mother as if she were a poor, deluded woman, insisting on finding out what had become of just one man.

Some years later, when I had found out everything about the death camps, I began to understand the significance of those looks of pity and the reasons why those people were unresponsive to my mother's pain. Why did she want to know? What made that one man so special that he alone should be remembered out of all the shadows of the damned in a hell they wanted to forget? She tried to make them remember, but they refused. They probably took part in that grim, pointless ritual just to get whatever my mother gave them. But who could blame them?

The more she became frustrated with those futile encounters, the more Mamma started to be sorry that they had transferred her brother out of Regina Coeli only a few weeks before the massacre at the Ardeatine Caves.[14] At first, while she still nurtured the hope that he might come back, she had been relieved that he had been taken out of Rome, but as hope faded she regretted that he didn't even have a grave over which she could grieve.

My mother died at the beginning of 1951, long before we were informed that Uncle Alberto had died in Auschwitz on the same day he arrived there, in early April 1944. She died after a long illness, and my father always maintained with absolute certainty that the first cell of the malignant tumour that killed her formed the very moment she heard that her brother had been arrested. Evidence of this was the fact that she immediately ran a high fever that couldn't be put down to anything else. Obviously, he has never been able to prove it. Even if he had, what good would it have done to acknowledge that the Nazis had succeeded in killing her too, some time after all the others?

The bond between my uncle and my mother had been very strong. Only many years later did I realise just how distraught she must have felt on hearing of his arrest: distraught to the point that she lost all judgement and

---

14. *Ardeatine Caves*: as a reprisal for a Resistance attack that had killed 42 German soldiers on the 23rd of March 1944, 335 Italian civilians were shot and buried in a sand cave near Rome on the following day.

allowed her husband and son to turn up at the head-quarters of the SS, attempting to wrest back prey from its captors. My mother loved her husband and son; it shocked me to think that her sorrow must have liter-ally driven her out of her mind.

The news of my uncle's arrest made saying goodbye to my parents and Guido even less bearable at the end of their visits.

One day I plucked up the courage to overcome the obedience they had instilled in me and asked my mother to take me away with her. I made my plea almost with-out hope that it would be listened to, but after a slight hesitation and an exchange of glances with my father, Mamma said, "Let's go and pack your case. You can stay with us till Sunday."

My parents' safe house was a flat in a little side street off the Lungotevere Flaminio, in one of the properties my father managed. Once again, the safe house was only safe thanks to the caretaker. The apartment was rented by a man who had gone north, to join the Republic of Salò. That's why it was empty and had to appear as such. Living in a vacant flat requires its own stringent rules: it is necessary to stay out as much as possible, to keep the windows shut at all times, and to observe the rule of silence, similar to that in an enclosed religious order. We kept all these rules: we spoke softly, especially near the entry door, and avoided making any sort of noise. Calling out to each other from one room to the next, for example, would have been an unforgivable mistake. Fortunately, the flat was on the first floor without anyone underneath, otherwise we would have needed the abil-ity to fly to avoid people hearing our footsteps.

Nearly all the tenants knew my father, who managed the building. He used to go in and out by himself, ahead of my mother and Guido, whom nobody knew. From the door of the apartment building, the caretaker, Amedeo Galimberti, a former *carabiniere*, would nod his head to indicate the coast was clear. If they did not see him nod, my parents would know to double back and try to enter the building again after a few minutes. A more definite shake of the head warned them to run quickly away in the opposite direction.

My family were not the only people the caretaker and his wife were hiding: the elegant apartment building was a safe house for about fifteen people. My father had no idea that the others were there. Only after the liberation of Italy did he find out, to his amazement, that there were generals, politicians and even a couple of Englishmen scattered throughout the building. To make the situation even more exciting, quite a few German officers visited the flat of a lady tenant, who was very generous with her favours.

With all those strict rules to observe, life in the flat couldn't be a lot of fun, but I wasn't aware of that on the day I arrived. That night everything seemed wonderful to me. Only much later did I realise how heavy those limitations were, but I also learned many ways of beating boredom, starting with reading. Papà had taught Guido how to play draughts, chess, and noughts and crosses; Guido quickly taught me so that he had an opponent who was more available and easier to defeat. My mother only read, as she had always loved doing.

I discovered other things about the secret life of that apartment building, but this came later, because I had to wait a long time for the joy of being reunited with my family for good. The happiness I felt on Friday nights, when they came to collect me from the Crespis', was as intense as the desolation I felt on Sunday afternoons, as the time to part again drew closer. In those hours nobody could soothe my pain; in the end, to put a stop to it, my parents decided to keep me with them. We were already taking a huge risk two days a week, what difference did a whole week make?

The anguish and desolation of those Sundays, as sunset drew near, have become a part of me. Even now, on Sunday afternoons, I am gripped by an uncharacteristic black mood and an anxiety that I never experience at other times, so I avoid going out and prefer to stay safely in my own home. I lie to myself, saying that the reason for my change of mood is the dislike that everyone feels for the coming Monday. I know that isn't the real reason I feel unsettled; I know what the feeling really stems from.

CHAPTER 11

By March I had won my battle: I was living with my family. We were all together, except for my sister, whom I hadn't seen since September, but now saw regularly. My father's initial caution had disappeared. Our family was almost completely reunited. The Americans were going to make a move eventually, but for how much longer was my father entitled to jeopardise a friend's life by asking him to hide me? I'd stayed with the Crespis for more than two months and on top of anything else, their fourth child was due any day.

Spring was coming, (even though winter seemed to go on forever that year). How much longer could the Germans go on defending Cassino? No one had any doubt about the final outcome of the war, even though a considerable part of Europe was still in Nazi hands. But the Italian front had stalled, and sadly the Red Army victories were still a long way off. Everyone just had to wait; but for us any wait could be one day too long…

Rome was too important a political objective for the Allies to delay much longer. Rome, the grown-ups said, would be the first step of their march – when spring came. But a European landing was also anticipated: who could guarantee that this strategy wouldn't sacrifice the Italian front in order to concentrate all forces in that huge push? Listening to these discussions I was introduced to strategy, which is perhaps less complicated than we are led to believe.

Nobody had any knowledge of what the Allies were planning. Not even my father, who was involved in the Resistance as a leading member of the Socialist Party, was in any better position to dispel the doubts that assailed us all. I don't know the details of what my father did in the Resistance because he never ever talked about it, either in those days or after the war, when many claimed to have been partisans. He didn't even ask for formal recognition of his activities as a Resistance fighter, when it became possible, even though he had been in charge of a section of Rome (although not as a military commander).

"I just did my duty," he always said.

Yet, he risked his life a number of times. Long after liberation, he let it slip that one day he was going down the stairs at a friend's flat after picking up a bundle of underground newspapers (I think it was the Socialist paper, *Avanti*), when he passed a squad of policemen on their way up to arrest his friend. He was always running around the city without us, and he wasn't taking care of his business, because he wasn't allowed to do his job. Later, others told me stories about my father's underground activities. They were stunned by my surprise, taking it for granted that he would have told me about them, and even exaggerated them, as everyone did afterwards.

My mother may also have done her bit for the Resistance, but I couldn't say for certain. What she did do was continually move around the city, and I don't think it was always to find something to eat on the black market. She met up with a lot of people apart from our relations, who were hiding out in several different homes. I never asked for explanations: one of the first things one learns in such situations is not to ask questions. It's not something that needs to be taught. Besides, I was just happy to hold on to my mother's hand and lose myself among the crowd, whom I observed carefully. I intuitively knew that among so many people in the street, a woman and two young boys were pretty safe. And in fact, nobody seemed to take any notice of us. However, we could never afford to lose concentration. One moment's carelessness might have meant the end for us.

Never stand out from the crowd; never do anything to attract attention for any reason whatsoever. We had to blend in with our surroundings, be invisible and not cause the slightest incident. An argument or a fight with anyone could have been fatal. And it was easy for something like that to happen, since we were living among frustrated, embittered people in conditions that bred aggression, even though they weren't in hiding as we were. Nearly everyone had a lined face, was quick to fly off the handle and was unnaturally thin; all signs of an exasperated population, among whom I hid for hours and hours every day. They were people full of rage and covered in scabies, which I picked up too, from getting on and off packed trams all day. (Treating it was easy: you just had to cover yourself all over in a foul-smelling ointment – the worst thing about it was having a bath in the evening, because there was no hot water and the flat wasn't heated).

What we feared most was the blind rage of those who knew their power was coming to an end and their fate was sealed. They were the most dangerous. Every uniform concealed a threat. When one suddenly appeared in front of me my heart missed a beat. I had made my own accurate ranking of their potential danger: German uniforms, of course, were the most frightening, especially the black SS ones; then those of their zealous servants, the *repubblichini* – soldiers of the Republic of Salò; then those of the Italian African Police with their anachronistic colonial style, a corps that was notorious for the fanaticism of many of its members. They were all potential enemies and the arrest of my uncle had made that danger painfully evident.

Thanks to my daily wanderings and my indiscriminate memory, I learned a lot of things that were strange and not particularly useful. I could list all the stops on the Red Circle Line and the Black Circle Line, two tramlines that ran around two different city loops. From the street names dedicated to the Risorgimento15. and figures from Italian history my mother taught me a little about Italy's past; that was one of the quirky aspects of my education that year. A touch of culture inspired by the streets that I travelled along by chance, and by the rules of survival as a fugitive in an extremely threatening environment surrounded by visibly unhappy, anxious and suspicious people, all potentially dangerous.

We trailed round and round the city. At lunch we sometimes met up with Papà. On those occasions we went to a restaurant. It would always be one of the best restaurants, where German officers ate (like *L'Amatriciana* opposite the Opera House). It was a

---

15. *Risorgimento*: the political and social movements between 1815 and 1870 which led to the unification of Italy, through international diplomacy, popular uprisings and three "wars of independence".

clever strategy: as far as we knew, there had never been a round-up in any of those expensive eating places. In addition, there was always a slightly higher chance of being offered a little extra on top of the meagre portions we could get with our ration cards, whose food stamps could be spent in restaurants too.

Our ration cards were, of course, forgeries. My father acquired the first ones with the disinterested help of a records office clerk, who had pretended to believe my father's yarn about his background and situation as an evacuee from the south. The clerk handed over the cards with a knowing look. This happened in the early months when checks were less strict, and Guido and I were away. Then the operation became more complicated, and my father wasn't able to obtain four cards which all had the same family name. That meant that two were in the name of "Giannini" and two in the name of "Coletti". I don't know what sort of alchemy was involved, but my mother appeared as my aunt.

"Make sure you don't forget," they'd remind me again and again, "If they ask you, remember to call Mamma 'Aunty'. You will remember, won't you?" I always answered "Yes" with absolute confidence, but I doubt that I would have kept up the pretence for long if I had ever been put to the test.

Rome was miserable, swept by an unrelenting, biting north wind. It was cold inside and outside the houses, which couldn't be heated. The electricity and gas were on for only a few hours each day. The black market fed nearly a million inhabitants, who sank into poverty as they sold off their family possessions in order to eat. They ran a huge risk, because sometimes the police arrested the profiteer and confiscated everything. At once, people had to find another supplier, then the precious new address was quietly passed on by women, to the few people dearest to them...

The trams were packed with short-tempered, smelly people. I used to wonder where all those people were going at all hours of the day. To their offices in the Ministries that had been shut down? Who knows, and yet so many people were on the move. It was winter and the acrid smell of smoke was everywhere, because all those able to find coal used it and their clothes reeked of it. Anything portable made of wood disappeared: park benches, planks from building sites, fences from around bombed areas, the branches of lots of trees...

The city was emptied by the curfew at sunset, which meant early afternoon in winter. Then darkness and blacked-out windows. Silence, hunger and cold, every night. And for us, the shared fear of hearing the doorbell ring...

CHAPTER 12

While I was staying at the Crespis', I hardly ever went out, but now that I was with my parents I spent all day outside. There was a regular pause in our wanderings at around two thirty every afternoon, when we visited the house where my sister was in hiding. At last I was able to see her again. Elena was staying with an old lady, who was the widow of a Signor Levi. Not being a Jew herself, she had been left undisturbed. Why would she, a lady in her nineties, have a little Jewish girl to help her and keep her company? So my sister was safe, but she still had her problems. Signora Penelope was lucid but not without her obsessions, which I soon became aware of. She lived in a luxurious apartment, much bigger than she needed, and we went there not just to see my sister, but for other important reasons.

The most pressing of these was to listen to Radio London, which broadcast in Italian at three o'clock every afternoon.16. A small group of regular listeners had begun to meet in that elegant and relatively safe flat. Each wore a mask of anxiety in the moments before the broadcast began, as they arranged the chairs

---

16. *Radio Londra*: Radio London was the name used for the BBC radio broadcasts to Italy between 1938 and the end of World War II. The broadcasts gave news about the progress of the war, countered Nazi and Fascist propaganda, and sent coded messages to Resistance units.

around the radio, kept at low volume for obvious reasons. A ring formed, sometimes bigger, sometimes smaller, of men and women leaning towards the imposing set, which was encased in wood and heavy fabric. The circle of anxious listeners religiously performed the ritual wait for good news – a ritual that was nearly always frustrating. They needed to tune the radio every time, finding their way through the interference broadcast from Germany – it would have been unwise to leave the set tuned to Radio London, since sudden police searches were always a risk.

"Tum-tum-te-te-te": the opening phrase of Beethoven's fifth symphony, which signalled the start of the broadcasts from Radio London, is engraved in the memory of all those who listened to it. Like me, none of them will ever forget it as long as they live. The news arrived every day with frustratingly little variation. Good news was still scarce and the disappointment was palpable. The Italian front was bogged down and only in Russia were things moving. But Russia was at the other end of the continent, and nothing was happening in Italy. And there was no sign of the second European front opening. Then there were messages in code which none of us could figure out.

We kids never listened right to the end of the broadcast because we had to do our school work. That was the third reason for our visits to Signora Penelope's. Another regular visitor was the teacher who had taught me the previous year and who now taught Guido, Elena and me the subjects we would have been studying if we could have gone to school.

My family came together every day in that apartment, which felt hospitable and hostile at the same time, but our time together was fleeting. My mother and father listened to the radio or talked politics; I could hardly talk to my sister because we were too busy with our lessons and homework. We could never squabble or even raise our voices in Signora Penelope's home. I was already in her bad books for not bowing to her when saying hello. And so our family reunions were only a mirage, with little more than a hug at the beginning and end of the brief period we spent together.

Sometimes I asked my mother for news of my old school friends, like Faccetta. She replied that she didn't know anything about him and that it was better not to go round asking questions. We were not to do anything that might let people know who we were, nothing that could link us to Jews. A mere suspicion could lead to our being picked up by the police for an identity check. Our papers were forged: we were supposed to have been evacuated from Avellino, but in less than two minutes any Italian could have worked out that we had never set foot there. So I had to keep my mouth shut. "When it's over, you'll find all of your friends again," she would comfort me. Nobody had told me about the round-up on the 16th of October. To what purpose? Talking about it would only have frightened me.

One morning on one of the usual outings with my mother, I found myself outside Rachel's block of apartments. I recognised it at once, and the caretaker knitting by the main door, sitting on a chair that was too small for her bulk.

"Mamma, let's ask about Rachel, maybe she still lives here."

"No, they're bound to have got away like us. And you know it's not safe to ask questions."

"What are you scared of? Tell the caretaker that we're friends just passing by," I insisted.

The caretaker didn't look in the least dangerous. That plump, stolid woman knitting away couldn't be a rabid Nazi. My mother finally agreed; she walked up to the woman, and feigning a superficial interest, asked about Rachel's family.

The caretaker looked her up and down and then glanced at me. I thought she seemed upset. She was surprised and I think she wanted to tell us something – maybe that we shouldn't go around asking questions. But she held back. She looked directly at my mother, as if her eyes were trying to communicate something her words could not.

"They don't live here anymore. The Germans took them away one morning in October. They haven't …come back yet. People say they've been taken up North."

The reference to October was clear to my mother, but not to me. How could it be possible? Poor Rachel, how could they have taken her away from her home?

"The Germans are taking the Jews…"

We stood there in silence for a few minutes. My right hand was squeezed in my mother's. With the other, I surreptitiously wiped my eyes every now and then. I was crying for Rachel, who I could still feel next to me at our school desk. I remembered the beginnings of our friendship. But most of all I was crying because I was scared – scared that we wouldn't make it and they would take us all away. I imagined the sound of the doorbell at our flat and the noise of the Germans' feet on the other side of the door, just like Rachel must have heard.

When I heard about my uncle's arrest I was sad, but not frightened: they'd caught him while he was doing something risky. But they had got to Rachel in her home, in her refuge, just like they could have got to us that very same evening. I felt something very like a foreboding. It was real and it hurt to the point of tears.

During the last weeks of the German occupation I got another scare. It was one of the few warm days I can recall in that period. All four of us were in a restaurant. People felt that liberation was close and perhaps this was why my father lowered his guard and broke two rules of caution. We were in a modest restaurant, right in the area where we lived. Someone might have recognised us and given us away.

We were eating when we heard the sudden screech of car brakes. A moment later, three German soldiers, armed to the teeth, barged into the restaurant and headed right for our table. My parents' faces went white; their hands gripped the tablecloth while the soldiers closed in on my right, coming up almost behind me. I felt a long, painful thud in my heart, as the four of us looked at each other, our eyes full of emotions that I will not even attempt to describe. But the soldiers went past our table without as much as a glance and headed into the kitchen. They soon came out again carrying bread rolls. I will never be able to describe how interminably long those seconds seemed.

Many years later, I was looking for a seat in a restaurant, a place that would allow me to sit with my back to the wall and see the door. It was something I had always done, something I always felt I had to do. I was bound by an old compulsion. Suddenly, I had a clear flashback to that scene in 1944 and realised where my curious habit had come from.

As I have said, I saw my sister nearly every day but only briefly. I was barely able to exchange two words with her, largely due to all the things we had to do, but also because Signora Penelope did not approve of Elena mixing with her ill-mannered brothers. She watched every move Elena made and all our contact with her while we were in the house. As far as the Signora was concerned, Guido and I were obstructing her intention to turn Elena into a proper young lady. She was right, I have to admit: we did not satisfy the standards of a lady educated in the middle of the nineteenth century.

But her ill opinion of our manners was not the most serious way the old lady made life difficult for Elena. Signora Penelope had a strong fixation that became a real problem, in fact an actual danger for my sister. The old lady was obsessed by the idea that food needed to be saved for "harder times", which quite frankly we had difficulty even imagining. Driven by that idea, she made Elena put something aside from the already meagre portions allowed by rationing, and from anything else that we were able to bring her. Nothing escaped the thorough search the woman carried out as soon as we had gone; everything ended up in the cupboard, under lock and key, and it nearly always stayed there until it went off. Then, with tears in her eyes, my sister had to throw out those invaluable provisions. Naturally, my parents were grateful to Signora Penelope for all she did for us, including Elena's education (right from the first day she only spoke to her in French, a language that a well-bred young lady needed to know). However, her senile obsession put my sister's health in jeopardy and she undoubtedly suffered from hunger more than any of us.

It goes without saying that Elena was never allowed outside with us, even for a short walk – "Because it's dangerous." My parents obeyed Signora Penelope's orders, to avoid disagreements, and also because, unfortunately, she was right. But we did try to break the embargo. I often had the job of slipping small parcels to Elena (it was easier to hide two small ones than one large one). Throughout our time in hiding, the success of those operations was my only contribution to any family member's fight for survival.

It was not as if we had food to throw away either: we were getting less and less with our ration cards as time went on. A hundred grams of bread a day isn't much. Seventy, which the ration was reduced to by the end of the war, was just crumbs to a growing boy. There was no meat to be had, just a few beans, maize flour, eggs and lots of *castagnaccio* – a cake made of nothing but chestnut flour, a dusting of sugar, a few pine nuts and some walnut pieces. Buying oil was like going to the goldsmith's and never has that dense, golden liquid from the Roman countryside so much resembled the precious metal.

I'd come back from Abruzzo fatter. I don't know how they'd managed it, but the Crespis had always given me enough to eat. At home, on the other hand, I was hungry. Malnutrition became evident when the first chilblains appeared on our hands and feet. These became open sores on our knuckles and our toes squeezed into our shoes. It wasn't the worst pain I've ever felt, but not the least either. In those days, without exception, boys of my age had to wear short trousers. Walking around in the cold north wind for many hours a day, it was impossible to avoid my thighs rubbing and becoming inflamed to the point of bleeding.

The evening meal we could expect was, to put it mildly, Spartan. On good nights, it was a bean soup cooked in the "cooking box." The cooking box was a miracle of make-do and used by everyone. It consisted of a wooden box in which even the tiniest gap was sealed. Inside, a space was left in the middle, just the right size to hold a cooking pot. All the surrounding space was filled with sawdust, wool and paper. The same lining was applied to the base and lid of the box, creating a perfectly heat-insulated container. In the morning, during the hour when the gas and electricity were on, the pan of beans was brought to the boil. While it boiled, it was put into the empty space in the box and the lid was closed. The whole thing was then wrapped in a blanket. In the evening, without any further need for a heat source, even the toughest chickpeas were cooked to perfection.

The problem was that often there were no beans to put in the pan and by the evening our few grams of bread were a forgotten memory, so dinner was just one egg and a little chicory.

CHAPTER 13

Until spring arrived and the curfew started later, I had to spend several long hours in silence when I came home in the evenings. Guido and I had to finish the homework started at Signora Penelope's, while Mamma and Papà usually read until dinner time.

The silence in that safe haven had an extraordinary, thrilling feel to it that I might even have enjoyed had it not lasted so long. Doing my school work was easy – after each day spent among the embattled people on the street and in the inhospitable home of Signora Penelope it was easy to think in that island of quiet. Silence has its own secret attraction. No one is ever quiet these days; voices and noises assail us from every direction all the time. And no one listens anymore, least of all to the countless voices of silence.

While we did our schoolwork, every now and again Guido would repeat out loud the odd Latin or even Greek sentence, to show just how much more important and difficult his work was than mine. I admired him and wondered if in a few years' time I too would be able to learn such difficult stuff. I also envied his exercise books with "single lines", because I was still writing between two, although the space between them was narrower than it had been the year before.

I had never particularly liked school, but during

those months I did my schoolwork willingly because it made life seem more normal. Everything else around me was hostile and dangerous, and far from normal. Only my school books and the third-grade syllabus made me feel that I was a part of ordinary life rather than a foreign body, an outsider, someone who was even hated. At that time I started to appreciate history, because it was the story of human beings; it was about events that were similar to the ones I was witnessing. It told stories about wars – big, important stories whose greatest appeal was that they had taken place in the past and could not make me feel guilty for being a passive bystander. Because that's how I felt about what was going on around me and what was happening to my family and the people I loved: a helpless victim, a defenceless spectator.

My occasional moments of intense fear were just the tip of the iceberg: distress, worry and a sense of powerlessness formed a heavy knot deep inside me that never went away.

I often found myself wishing that I were not just a boy of seven, always having to hold someone's hand, a helpless observer of things I had to endure but didn't understand: I wanted to be a man.

Once I did try to "be a man". I was on a tram and two German soldiers caught my eye. Perhaps they had made an impression on me because they looked so young: one of them could only have been Guido's age – fourteen, or not much older. I stared at them full of hostility, but one of them gave me a warm smile, tinged with homesickness: maybe I had reminded him of a little brother. I was desperate for action and needed an outlet. I was determined to do something, but either that smile or my cowardice, or both, held me back. I planned to spit at their feet while looking them in the eyes, as I imagined a man would have done…but I just spat, without any look of defiance, without even meeting their eyes. Instead of a proud little hero, I just looked like an ordinary, uncouth Italian. I could tell that from their amused looks, which showed no trace of offence.

In spring the Americans landed in Anzio, which is only about sixty kilometres from Rome, with no natural barrier in between. Like everyone else, for several days we felt entitled to hope that they would soon reach Rome and free us. That didn't happen, because the army didn't follow the reconnaissance patrol. We later learned that on the day of landing this patrol reached the outskirts of Rome without meeting a single German soldier.

Once that dream faded, we gave up hope of hearing the pounding of the guns, announcing the arrival of the Allied troops. Dejectedly we went back to listening to Radio London, which kept my parents in suspense with its endless refrain about "clashes between patrols on the Anzio front". This came after all the other news, as if Rome were the least important of the war objectives.

Yet more afternoons spent at Signora Penelope's – and they were even longer now that the curfew didn't start until seven o'clock. And yet more endless, unbearable weeks, while salvation seemed within our reach.

But then, towards the end, time seemed to speed up: the final offensive was about to begin. My father was increasingly involved in working for the party, and was coming home later and later, often after curfew. He was also spending much less time with us in the afternoons.

Liberation was in the air, but this made us more scared. It was easy to let one's guard down and behave carelessly, fooled by the feeling that salvation was near.

Maybe it was carelessness that betrayed Eugenio Colorni, one of my father's comrades and friends, or maybe it was just bad luck that a couple of Republic of Salò militiamen recognised him in the street. They lay in wait until he came out of a doorway and then gunned him down. "They shot him in cold blood, like a rabid dog in the middle of the street," my father told my mother, "in Via Livorno, without even arresting him." A pointless, senseless murder for no other reason than to give vent to their anger, knowing their days to be numbered. It was as if they were retaliating against the guns, which could finally be heard thundering from the hills south-east of Rome. They used poor Colorni to release their frustration only a few hours away from liberation.

That was the first time I ever saw my father cry – in anger as well as pain. "Now, with the Allies at the gates!" he kept repeating, distraught, tearing his hair, unable to calm down.

My mother was in a state of constant, growing fear, but for our sake and her own she stuck to the routines and rhythms of our gypsy-like existence on the run, which seemed to never end.

CHAPTER 14

On the afternoon of the 4th of June we went to see my sister, unaware that it would be the last time we would visit her as people in hiding. My father wasn't with us. Somehow word had got around that public transport would not be operating from the afternoon onwards, and so Mamma and I started walking home earlier than usual. We set off well before six, because we had a long way to go.

Our route took us across Via Salaria, and there, for the first time in so long, I savoured the taste of freedom. We saw the Germans on the run. The convoy was endless: trucks, buses and guns being towed by a variety of vehicles, armoured cars and tanks. The soldiers filed by in orderly ranks, silently and visibly exhausted. A few people waiting to cross the road watched in silence; they tried to catch the eyes of the soldiers, who were looking away. Their eyes were downcast and there was no sign of the arrogance shown towards Rome and the Romans in the preceding months. Our eyes were quite different – they were brimming with happiness, relief and hope. Our silence was a shout of joy, which we only suppressed for fear of an angry response from the enemy. My mother whispered excitedly, over and over again, "They're going, they're going, now they're going!"

After a long wait, we were able to cross Via Salaria between two sections of the interminable convoy. We set off on our way again, but I can't remember walking: I was so happy I must have been floating several centimetres above the ground. When we came to Via Flaminia we met another military convoy that was shorter than the first. "They're going, they're going!" The streets were deserted now, because people feared a sudden last strike from the retreating army. We just continued walking and being alone allowed us to enjoy the moment more intensely.

We finally arrived home. The caretaker was there, just like any other evening, watchful and cautious as usual. This time, my mother plucked up her courage and stopped to talk to him at the main doorway. Without hiding her joy, she excitedly described to him what we had just seen.

My father wasn't at home; he had let us know that he wouldn't be back that night. My mother's concern for him was the only shadow over her joy, apart from the sadness for her lost brother. It was rumoured that the Germans were going to blow up the bridges and she thought, not without good reason, that Papà might have gone out to try and stop them. We were so incredibly excited that we were unable to stick to the usual safety rules. My mother went up and down stairs too many times, coming and going from the caretaker's lodge. Eventually, I fell asleep.

Early next morning, we were woken by the unusual noise of engines and voices, coming from the street. For a while my mother held back, but then she couldn't help herself and raised the blinds. It was the first time she had looked from a window in that block of flats, after eight months of living there.

"Americans!" she shouted, turning back into the room and hugging us, "They're Americans!" We children raced to the window after her: looking to our left we could see military vehicles that were quite different to those we were used to, driving down the Lungotevere Flaminio. The soldiers were different too. People cheered them on and they responded to the kisses sent by the crowds on either side of the street. A few moments later, delirious with happiness, we joined those people.

My father had been out that night, but he was not in any particular danger. The Germans did not try to blow up the bridges of Rome. Aunt Amelia and Yvonne, who had been hiding in the San Lorenzo district in south-eastern Rome, saw the Americans arrive just as we were watching the Germans leave the city on Via Salaria. When I found this out I was envious of their extra night of freedom.

Two years later, Yvonne died – a late victim of the Nazi occupation. Her weak constitution was unable to withstand the extreme cold and malnutrition during that winter. She suffered a relapse of the illness from which she had recovered right at the beginning of the war. She died in April, 1946, when people had already started to talk about a drug that could cure TB. My gentle cousin, who passed away at the age of twenty-five, was one of the last victims of the war and of an illness that nowadays barely rates a mention.

CHAPTER 15

If I examine how my memory works, I notice that up to the 8th of September 1943, it recorded images like a still camera. In my mind there are snapshots of family life, games, my first year at school, bomb raids, air-raid shelters and lots of other things. They are frozen images of specific moments.

From the late afternoon of that day, in their place there is a sequence of memories, like a film, which I have tried to "project" in the previous pages. The film proceeds slowly, as if the reel were having trouble unwinding. The prevailing colour in all the scenes is dark grey. The almost constant sensation is one of cold. Equally constant is the feeling of emptiness and deprivation, due to the scarcity of food, especially bread. In the film of those days there is also another underlying lack of nourishment, that of the spirit: being untroubled, being carefree, laughter, childhood games, the racket all children are entitled to make at that age.

From the day of liberation onwards, my memories start coming off the reel faster – very much faster. Images overlap and juxtapose as if the spring on the projector has snapped and the film is unwinding madly. I see everything at crazy speeds, like a Buster Keaton film…

People partying in the streets of Rome, our family

among them. Going back to our own home, all together again, Aunt Amelia and Yvonne included. The much longed-for return of our radio. The entrance test for admission to Grade 4 in September. Then having to share the school building with American soldiers for an entire year. Being in one class, together with all the other children, no longer apart or discriminated against. Studying a map of Europe with my father, who is pointing to the places where the Allied troops are advancing and showing me how the black Nazi stain is shrinking. The parcels sent by American Jews, full of unfamiliar food and clothes of a style and colour that seem unreal. A few more trips with my mother to buy things on the black market, but what we buy now is no longer essential to survival. The end of the war in Europe. The atomic bomb that everyone was talking about…

The images pile up, a little blurred and confused, because each races after the one before. I have tried to sort them out, to give them a connecting thread. The sun is present in all these scenes, lighting them up and warming them. The cold has gone; the oppressive grey of those cursed nine months has gone.

One more memory comes up to join these images. One morning, while leafing through the paper, I came across the news reporting that Scarpato, the informer who had given Uncle Alberto away, had been executed. I announced it to everyone, proud of what I had found out, but soon afterwards we stopped caring: his death brought us no joy, nor did it bring my uncle back.

I have wondered why my memory moves at different speeds. Most of all, I have wondered why the memories of the period of Nazi occupation move so slowly. I believe that the pace of the other memories is normal, considering my age at the time and the speed of events. The most plausible explanation I can find is that during the occupation we survived "by the skin of our teeth". Our life was exhausting, full of fear and anxiety, and every day we just tried to make it through to the evening. Every night we fell asleep afraid of the dark and the silence, which might be broken by the sound of someone at the door. The thought that we might be betrayed by an informer was constant, always there in our subconscious. Often I was struck by images of someone being caught: myself or one of the people close to me, or the people who were far away and whose fate I did not know, as had happened when I was in Abruzzo. I think that the slow pace of these memories is a consequence of just how difficult our life was in that period.

I have wondered to what extent I have been marked by the deep anxiety and fear that I might not make it – which was intensified on hearing that Rachel had been taken away. I have frequently dreamt of being pursued, that someone wanted to capture me. I'm not sure whether this dream could be described as a "recurring" one. It doesn't matter. The dream has never really been frightening, let alone a nightmare. It feels like a difficult moment, requiring all my concentration, all my intelligence and a great degree of self-control, but I always know I am going to make it and nobody is going to catch me. A couple of times, the mood has even been playful, because I was confident that I would get the better of my pursuers. These people have never worn a uniform, be it German, or Fascist, or even of the Italian African Police.

Life bared its teeth at me in the beginning. Among the first images in my album of memories are the time we were expelled from a seaside resort, the day they seized our radio, which meant much more to us in those days than a television would today, no longer being invited to play at another boy's house because I was Jewish, my school report for the year 1942-43 with "Of the Jewish Race" written on it in red and the burden of feeling different and despised. These are the photos in my first album, juxtaposed with others, photos of a normal life, with memories of a normal family. And then there's the "film" of the months of German occupation, with its victims – people I loved.

Among my memories there are people who, for a few thousand lire or a few litres of black market oil, sent their fellow Italians, including my uncle, to certain death. But there are also people who risked their own lives to save ours: the records office clerk who – in exchange for a look of gratitude – gave my father the ration cards that allowed him and my mother to eat; the Fascist Party official who hurried to warn my father of the impending threat to Jews as the Germans entered Rome; there is even an SS captain, not entirely stripped of humanity by his cursed uniform, who spared the lives of my father and brother, two Jews who stepped into his headquarters.

I lived under the threat of terrifying, hostile forces that my parents could never attempt to fight, only evade. I lived with the knowledge that if we were caught, they would be unable to defend me.

All this happened to me. If I had not had memories to counteract the devastating effects of these experiences – memories of those people who rescued us – and if I had miraculously survived without their help, I would have grown up full of hate. Everyone around me would have looked like a pack of growling dogs, like the ones Rachel probably saw right before the end. If that has not happened, if I have been left with any moral sense, it is due to those selfless individuals.

What I went through at that time has taught me, more effectively than any preacher could have done, that no one should pass judgement on others on the basis of their origins, religion, class, politics, country of birth, or any other label that fate has attached to them. A meal of polenta spread on a table from which everyone eats has taught me that we must consider the rights of others as well as our own needs. Life has confirmed these intuitions, born of my experiences during those nine, very long months.

That is why I am the product of my memories, flecks of dust in the whirlwind of those terrible times, just as what happened to me is an atom of history.